MW01121856

Aesop's Secret
By Claudia White

AESOP'S SECRET

BY CLAUDIA WHITE

MP PUBLISHING

First edition published in 2013 by
MP Publishing Limited
6 Petaluma Blvd. North, Suite B6, Petaluma, CA 94952 USA
and
12 Strathallan Crescent, Douglas, Isle of Man IM2 4NR British Isles
mppublishingusa.com

White, Claudia.
Aesop's secret / by Claudia White.
p. cm.
ISBN 978-1-84982-230-5
Summary : Melinda and Felix Hutton discover they're part of an
ancient race of shape-shifters, the Athenites. They must fight to defend
their family – and their race – against forces that would destroy them.

[1. Mythology, Greek --Fiction. 2. Shapeshifting --Fiction. 3. Family
--Fiction. 4. Siblings --Fiction. 5. Fantasy fiction.] I. Title.

PZ7.W58249 Ae 2013
[Fic] --dc23

Jacket Design by Iain Morris
Jacket Image by Larissa Kulik

ISBN-13: 978-1-84982-230-5
10 9 8 7 6 5 4 3 2 1

Also available in eBook

To Samantha and Ian, who happily listened to every version of the story in its development, and to Oakie, my four-legged, furry best friend.

Everyone is different, so in a sense we're all similar...

CHAPTER ONE

"Felix, stop it!" Melinda screamed at her twelve-year-old brother, who was jumping around and around her. Felix ignored her as he danced in a circle, trapping her from getting away. "Stop it! I'm telling Mom you're acting like an ape!"

Felix hadn't touched her and wasn't talking to her. He simply danced around her, bending low to the ground, grunting and jumping up, throwing his arms above his head. Melinda wanted him to stop but the more she yelled the more he danced.

Felix continued his ritual-like behavior, turning and jumping, around and around. Melinda stared out through a waterfall of tears. This wasn't Felix's normal serious behavior. His idea of a good time was usually reading or conducting scientific experiments. He never teased his sister. In fact, he never did much of anything with her. He was changing, and not only his personality. His thin face was widening; his forehead became swollen, looking like a ledge over his eyes that seemed to be sinking into his face. His glasses fell to the floor when the bridge of his thin nose flattened against his face and his nostrils flared shockingly wide. His upper lip was longer from his nose down to his chin, and his chin was getting smaller. The next turn his cheeks sank into his face and his cheekbones looked like chiseled shelves under his eyes. Another turn and Felix's face was hairy—not a beard like on a grown man, his whole face was hairy.

Melinda burst into laughter. One more turn and Felix no longer looked like a boy at all. Melinda still had tears rolling down her face but now from hysterical laughter. Felix's behavior wasn't the only ape-like thing about him because now he even looked like a big hairy ape dancing and grunting, and swinging his now very long arms. Melinda laughed so hard she fell to the ground.

"WOULD YOU JUST SHUT UP?" Felix snarled.

"You look like an orangutan!" Melinda laughed.

"Yeah, and you're an idiot girl! Melinda, wake up…I'm sick of your stupid dreams, it's five in the morning!" Felix pushed on Melinda's shoulder until she opened her eyes. He was himself again, and she was in bed. She'd had another dream.

Felix left the room, slamming the door behind him. Melinda was still giggling, thinking about Felix as an ape-boy. What made it extra funny was that in real life her brother never had the charms of a chimp.

Melinda lay back on her pillow and smiled. She had been having a lot of great dreams lately. In all these dreams someone had changed in an extraordinary way. One night she had sprouted feathers and wings and had flown over the top of their house. Another night she had developed a blowhole and flippers and swam with dolphins in the surf. One time she and her mother had both transformed into giraffes so that they could retrieve a kite in a tree. Night after night, her subconscious granted her another wonderful transformation and, so far, she'd never changed into the same creature twice.

Melinda wished she had someone to share her dreamy adventures with. She had told her family all about them but they didn't seem very interested. Aesop, her pet rabbit, didn't appear to be either. Unfortunately, she didn't have any friends because they'd just moved again. In Melinda's ten years, they'd moved seven times.

Now they lived near the city of Seattle in America. Their house in the countryside was surrounded by dairy farms. It was a big, old house with a big secluded garden. It should have been the ideal place to grow up, but Melinda was lonely and knew they'd probably move again before long because her mother, Elaine, was an author and was researching a book about myths and folklore. The family accompanied her wherever she needed to go; Melinda's father Jake (who was qualified as a doctor and veterinary surgeon) worked in local hospitals and animal clinics wherever they moved. Melinda had never known anything else and it had never bothered her before now.

The truth was that more than wanting to share her dream world with someone, Melinda wished the dreams were real. She wished she could really fly, swim like a fish or gallop like a horse.

"It would be fun to be a horse," she sighed as she kicked off her covers.

The sun was already shining brightly and Melinda was wide awake, so even though it was still very early she dressed, raced downstairs and galloped outside into the back garden.

The early morning air was cool and dew still clung to the grass. Birds chirped eagerly in their hunt for breakfast while insects dashed around, trying to avoid becoming their morning meal. In the distance a rooster crowed and a crow cawed. The early morning buzz of activity was everywhere.

At the back of the garden was a fence separating their garden from the dairy farm's grazing land. Melinda liked to visit the cows as they grazed lazily. Their gentle faces and liquid brown eyes seemed so peaceful. But there were no cows at this time of the morning, only the soft sound of mooing from the milking barn at the other side of the field. Melinda looked out across the field; a sea of golden grasses swayed silently. She imagined herself as a sleek gazelle leaping toward the horizon.

A breeze brushed her curly brown hair into her eyes, a reminder that she was simply a short, slightly pudgy ten-year-old girl with freckles playing connect the dots across her face. She sighed, hoisted herself over the bottom rung of the fence and ran as fast as she could to the top of a small rise in the center of the field.

On the far side of the field the cows, having finished in the milking parlor, were on their way back to graze. One especially large cow looked in Melinda's direction. Melinda waved wildly with both arms, motioning it to come to her. Seeming to oblige, the cow walked haltingly toward her. It stopped, lowered its head, then began to trot, never taking its eyes off of Melinda.

As the cow drew closer, Melinda realized, to her horror, that this bovine was no cow. It was a bull! Her heart burst into violent throbs. She gulped in a lungful of air then turned and ran. The bull ran too, in fact he appeared to be charging, with his head lowered, his eyes glaring and steam clouds billowing out of his nose and mouth.

Melinda ran with more speed than she had ever mustered before, all the while wishing that her dreams were real—if they had been she would change into a horse and gallop away. She thought of nothing else as the bull charged, closing the gap between them with every one of his powerful strides.

In her dream she'd run with horses, now she was running for her life. She imagined herself as a strong thoroughbred flying across the field. Faster and faster she galloped away from the bull, racing toward the fence, racing to safety. She was so engrossed in her fantasy that she didn't notice when the bull stopped, lowering his head as he pawed the ground. She didn't notice him snort one last puff of steam then resume grazing as if he hadn't a care in the world.

Oblivious to everything except the exhilaration of the speed she had managed, Melinda raced on, imagining how a horse must feel with its hooves beating the ground, nostrils open wide, tail held high. When she reached the fence she kicked off the ground and sailed easily over.

Stunned by the feat but still very wary of the bull, she spun around, expecting to see it skidding to a halt inside the fence. Her stomach tightened when she saw the tip of his tail swoosh around in back of her, shockingly on her side of the fence. She darted forward; the sound of hooves was alarmingly close. She glanced around in back of her again, catching another glimpse of the tip of that tail as it flicked through the air.

Every muscle in her body quivered and her stomach knotted painfully as she tried to outrun the bull again, but no matter how fast or how far she ran the sound of those hooves stayed right with her, the flash of that tail always only inches away. Terror replaced her fear as she prepared for the bull's attack.

He was obviously very close yet mysteriously hidden from view. No matter which way she turned she couldn't see his massive form, his frightening head, his angry eyes or the sight of his powerful legs and crushing hooves…until she looked down and saw them directly below her.

She leapt backward with incredible force. They followed, landing when she did. They moved forward when she did. They moved backward when she did. They jumped when she did. No matter when, where, or how fast she moved, those hooves did the same thing at the same time and at the same speed.

Curiosity was quickly replacing fear as those hooves seemed to respond to her every command. It was at that moment that she began to realize the two things that would change her life forever. First she realized that those hooves were not bull's hooves at all but rather horse's feet. The second thing was that her feet were nowhere in sight.

"I'm still dreaming," she laughed aloud, emanating what sounded more like a whinny than a giggle. "I'M A HORSE!" she called loudly to anyone else whom she might have conjured up for this particular fantasy.

Felix hadn't slept well after Melinda's rude awakening. He rolled over and glimpsed the lighted dial of his clock; it was 6:30 a.m.

"At least I got a little more sleep," he sighed. He rolled onto his back—unable to sleep anymore, but not keen to get up. Groaning in anger, he thought about Melinda and how he hadn't had a good night's sleep in weeks because of her ridiculous dreams.

It was pointless to stay in bed so he went to the window to examine the day's weather prospects. "Well at least it's going to be a good one," he said with a stretch, noting the clear blue sky stretching out for as far as he could see. "I doubt if even Melinda can ruin this." Then movement at the back of the garden caught his eye. "You've got to be kidding," he gasped, then shouted, "Mom, Dad, come here quickly—you've got to see this!"

His father stumbled into the room. "What's wrong?" he slurred through a wide yawn, as he adjusted his dark-rimmed glasses onto the bridge of his nose. His pale face was dark with the stubble of his unshaven beard.

Elaine, struggling to find the armholes of her dressing gown, came in behind. Barely awake, she looked confused, her long red hair knotted and sticking out in every direction.

They hadn't reached the window when Felix turned, a bemused smile curling his lips. "Melinda is in the back garden...and she's naked!"

CHAPTER TWO

"I can't believe it," Elaine cooed, "our baby is growing up." She smiled in a motherly kind of way. She looked over at Jake, sighing happily. "We should have suspected something with all those dreams."

"Yep," Jake said with a smile, "but it is awfully early."

Felix squinted at his parents. "What are you talking about? Melinda is out in the garden at 6:30 in the morning, stark naked, and you're acting like…like…well, like she's done something to be proud of!"

Jake laughed, squeezing Felix's arm and jerking his head toward the doorway. "Let's go get your sister. I think it's time that you both learn a bit more about the facts of life."

Felix was sprawled on the sofa in the living room when Elaine and Jake walked in with Melinda. He watched with disgust as his mother hugged and fussed over his sister as if she'd just taken her first step or said her first word. Melinda, wrapped snugly in a blanket, looked dazed as she was ushered into the room and then made comfortable on the large blue chair in front of the fireplace.

"I had this weird dream where I was a horse," Melinda chattered. "There was this bull and…" she paused as she looked around at the faces of her family. "I must have been sleepwalking but…" Her voice trailed off.

Elaine smiled and shook her head. "Don't you remember going outside? Do you remember what happened to you?"

Felix's mouth seemed to be fixed into a permanent snarl as Melinda nodded, then explained everything from when she left the house until she wandered back into the garden.

Jake and Elaine looked proudly at their daughter. Jake cleared his throat and for the first time in his life looked a little embarrassed. "Well then, it looks like what I think is happening…*is*. In which case your mother and I need to prepare you both for all the exciting changes that your body will be going through; it's time that you know about the facts of our lives."

Felix and Melinda looked at each other blankly, both remembering the "facts of life" lecture they had already received from their no-nonsense father.

Jake continued, "Elaine, why don't you tell the kids who we are."

Both Jake and Elaine seemed unusually giddy about the subject that, after a deep breath, Elaine launched into. "Human beings are very superstitious. There has always been hatred and discrimination against people who are different. Because of blind hatred, a lot of real history is disguised in stories. There are a lot of stories, myths, fables and folktales that are clever representations of the human imagination. Others are based on real historical facts—some may surprise you. Over the centuries, almost all of these factual stories have been discounted as imaginative tales. It's an important part of history that has been ignored."

Felix's snarling lips were now accompanied by a bug-eyed disbelieving stare. "What does any of this have to do with the facts of life, let alone the reason for Melinda's Lady Godiva impersonation out in the garden?"

Elaine sighed. "It's all rather complicated…I don't know how to explain what is happening to Melinda without telling you both about your heritage. If I don't tell you everything, you'll be even more confused than you are now. I want you to learn about our history because we are unique. Our people are the subject of a lot of stories and it's because of superstition and persecution that we are. For centuries we have been forced to live secret lives, never letting anyone know who and what we really are. We are different and therefore at risk."

What we really are? Melinda's face screwed up at the thought. *Mom must be crazy…that would definitely explain a lot of things.*

Felix turned his thoughts away from what he considered to be an absurd discussion. *Luckily I got my brains from Dad—at least I hope I did.*

Elaine looked to be at a loss for words for an instant, then as if struck with inspiration, she continued. "I want you both to think about some of the stories I've read to you. Look around the room at some of the art pieces we've collected from around the world. Look at this one." Elaine held up a small white marble sculpture they had brought back from Greece years before. The statue was of the god Zeus and his daughter, the goddess Athena. Athena was changing into some kind of bird. "Remember the story about the game Zeus and Athena played where they changed into all those animals? Zeus tricked Athena into changing into something very small so that he could capture her and keep her all to himself?"

"I remember that one," Melinda said proudly. "She changed into a fly and he swallowed her so that she would live in his brain and advise him."

"Well done, that's right," Elaine smiled.

Felix's face distorted into a grotesque caricature of himself. "What does this have to do with anything?"

Elaine ignored him. "Remember the story called *Limpet Rock*?" she asked, pointing to a small carving of a seal that sat on the table closest to Felix. "That little statue reminded me of the Celtic folktale about the seal who turned into a girl."

"I remember that one too…A man found her when she shed her seal skin and became a human woman. He fell in love with her then hid her seal skin so that she would have to stay with him and be his wife," Melinda said seriously.

Elaine nodded. "I think you understand the kind of story I'm talking about…in each of these tales, people changed into something else. Melinda, I'll bet they're like your dreams aren't they?"

Melinda nodded. Felix rocked his head back on the sofa in disgust. "This is stupid—it doesn't have anything to do with me, can I go?"

"I'm afraid it does have everything to do with all of us. This is all about the changes that you two will both experience," Jake said sternly.

Elaine looked at the figurines, paintings, and sculptures of mythological creatures she had collected over the years. There were winged horses, bull-headed men, and dancing half-man, half-goat creatures everywhere. She needed another prop to help her in her explanation but when she looked into the faces of Melinda and Felix she knew that this tactic wasn't working. "OK, this is more difficult than I thought. Let's try something else," she said almost to herself. "I want you both to close your eyes and imagine what a seal might feel like. Try to sense what it would be like to be in the water and experience the excitement of gliding through the surf, darting after fish as you dive weightlessly into the depths of the sea."

Felix didn't understand what his mother wanted from him. He barely remembered any of the stories she used to read to him. He knew he had enjoyed listening to them when he was a lot younger but that was a long time ago. He couldn't *feel* anything about the stories and he couldn't see anything in his memory except his mother sitting with him and reading aloud.

Melinda closed her eyes. It was easy to see and sense how the water would feel rippling over a seal's sleek body. She visualized herself turning from a girl into a seal.

"That's enough," Elaine said so abruptly that Melinda jumped while Felix's frown deepened.

Felix looked from his mother to his father, both of whom looked like something miraculous had occurred. He turned to see if Melinda understood what was meant to have happened and shuddered.

Her face looked grossly different. Her skin was gray and her eyes seemed almost black. He rubbed his eyes with an involuntary shiver and looked back at her. She looked like she always did, cheerful and clueless in his opinion. Everything seemed normal, and should have felt the same, but Felix was uncomfortable.

Jake smiled proudly. "Well done, Melinda. I'll bet you feel terrific."

Melinda smiled weakly. She had no idea how her father knew about the exhilarating sensations she had just experienced but he certainly seemed to.

"Felix, did you feel anything different?" his mother asked cautiously.

A corner of Felix's lips curled unpleasantly as he shook his head.

Jake cleared his throat. "I don't have a medical explanation for what's happening to Melinda: she is growing up rather quickly." He turned his attention to Felix. "Felix, you are not going through the same changes yet but you will soon. Our bodies usually start to mature at around fourteen or fifteen, not at age ten like in Melinda's case."

Felix's head was pounding. "I still don't know what you're talking about. All I know is that I woke up to see Melinda standing out in the garden without anything on, then you and Mom start talking nonsense about myths and maturity. WHAT'S GOING ON?"

Jake massaged his forehead with one hand while his other hand massaged the back of his neck. When he was finished he took a deep breath, exhaled slowly then met Felix's frustrated gaze. "We are descendants of a race of people known as Athenites. We believe the name is connected to the goddess Athena because of her ability to metamorphose into different creatures. To be honest I don't know whether we were named after her, or she was named after us, but that doesn't really matter. What does matter is that you know who you are and what you can do. It appears that Melinda has already experienced transformations. This morning her survival instincts allowed her to escape from the charging bull by transforming into a horse. It's what Athenites have always been able to do throughout history, calling on the strengths of another creature to survive. And what we just witnessed here confirms that she is indeed maturing as her mind focused on becoming a seal and she nearly succeeded in changing into one," he said proudly.

Felix sat dumbfounded. If his mother had said all of this he wouldn't have believed her—she was always talking about fables and their connection to reality. He usually ignored her. Then it dawned on him: this was all a joke…a hoax designed to get Melinda to stop all her babbling about changing into animals. "OK," he laughed, "If we can transform then show us how it's done."

"Are you sure you're ready for this?" Elaine cautioned.

"Sure," Felix answered cheerfully. "If it's our destiny then let's see what's in store for us."

Jake looked more animated than usual, almost like a child picking out a favorite toy. "All right, let's see, what will it be?" He closed his eyes and froze his movements. His breathing was subtle and steady. His dark beard was growing rapidly, turning from brown to gray and now covered his face. On the top of his head, pointy ears sprouted, growing straight up like a dog's. His nose flattened and both his mouth and jaw elongated, ballooning straight out from his face. His whole body was changing rapidly. His shoulders became narrower, then they expanded as his neck grew thicker. Clothes that minutes before fit perfectly now seemed too large as they hung on his fur-covered body. His eyelids lifted to reveal round, yellow-brown eyes. He hoped to see understanding and acceptance, maybe even enthusiasm on the faces of his children.

He got all three from Melinda. Her excitement was barely contained. She looked like she wanted to try the transformation herself.

Felix looked horrified as he stared at the wolf in his father's clothing. He had turned a ghostly white. His mouth hung open as he gasped for breath. He looked like he might faint, throw up, or both. Instead, he stood up, moved backward, then ran out of the room and out of the house.

CHAPTER THREE

The only word to describe Felix's behavior over the next two weeks was polite. He exhibited extraordinary courtesy to everyone in his family, even Melinda. He didn't talk to them any longer it took to ask or answer a simple question but he no longer grunted his morning greeting. Instead he would politely say the words "Good morning." When his mother set his dinner plate in front of him, he gave her a gracious, "Thank you," and when he decided to leave a room he said things like, "I hope you'll excuse me, I need to see to some things." Felix had become a courteous stranger in his own home.

Jake's reaction to his son's behavior was simple: "The boy will get things organized in his mind in his own way and his own time. We need to give him some space to adjust."

Elaine worried anyway. "I never thought he would react to his ancestry this way."

Melinda didn't see the problem. "I don't see what the big deal is," she offered. "At least he's polite." She couldn't be bothered with her brother's mood. She was still reeling with excitement from the discovery of her new talents and used every opportunity to nag her parents into helping her learn how to use them properly. Unfortunately they never had the time, so she had to experiment on her own.

The weather had changed into something Seattle was famous for: patchy drizzle and otherwise gray conditions. It didn't matter to Melinda as she prepared to transform into a squirrel. Her model was the gray squirrel that resided in the tall oak tree at the back of the garden. She walked out to the middle of the lawn and stripped off her clothes, knowing from experience that when an Athenite transforms their clothes don't. The cold air almost stung as it hit her skin so she acted quickly, closing her eyes and freezing her movements, concentrating on the image of the small rodent that she had observed earlier that day. As the familiar tingling of transformation spread throughout her body she heard the caw from a crow in the distance and for a split second visualized its shiny black feathers. As quickly as the image arrived, she shoved it aside and let squirrels be her sole focus. Fleetingly she remembered that her father always called them bushy-tailed rats.

The back door slammed loudly startling Melinda out of her trance. Her eyes sprang open and she saw that her clothes were now looming high above her. Then, in a more startlingly observation, she noticed a pair of huge shoes coming rapidly toward her.

Having seen Melinda's clothes from inside the house, Felix had gone to investigate. He could not allow her to leave her things here, there, and everywhere with the impending arrival of Professors

Mulligan and Stumpworthy. They were due to arrive any day and he had to make a good impression.

A few weeks before Felix was confronted with what he referred to as "Athenite insanity," he had received an invitation to attend the prestigious Stumpworthy School of Science in Paris, France. He had dreamed about attending that school since he was six years old. Excited beyond belief, he began the persuasion process on his parents that he hoped would convince them to let him go. At the time they seemed to be as thrilled as he was about the possibility. His mother even knew a member of the governing board: an old colleague and friend named James Mulligan. He and Horace Stumpworthy, the owner of the school, were currently traveling around the world to meet prospective students, and his parents had happily invited them to come to their home and meet Felix.

But then Melinda ruined everything. Ever since her changes began, his parents were of two minds about whether or not he should be allowed to study so far away from home. His mother was reluctant to let him go. "Maybe next year would be better," she had moaned. "There are so many changes going on right now, it would be wise to wait." While his father offered slightly more encouragement: "Let's see how things go with Mulligan when he visits, then make up our minds."

The last couple of weeks had been a nightmare. Most mornings Felix awoke feeling as he did before learning the facts of his life. However, things quickly soured when greeted by his bubbling, unpredictable sister. One morning he had to do a double-take when he saw that she had long furry ears on top of her head; another morning she had a big, black bushy tail dragging on the floor from underneath her dressing gown. A boy at his school had always referred to his little sister as a pig. Felix shuddered to think what would happen if he called his sister a pig.

"It's normal when you're maturing to suffer unexpected transformations," his father had explained. "If your mind wanders your body follows. You have all this to look forward to."

Felix could honestly say that he was NOT looking forward to experiencing any of the changes that his sister was already going through because transforming didn't interest him in the least. As the days passed his resolve to never morph out of his own body and into another creature strengthened. But he knew that the only way to avoid becoming like the other mutants in his family was to go away. So he made up his mind: whatever it took, he was going to that school, and the sooner the better.

Grumbling under his breath, he reached Melinda's clothes, hastily picked them up then headed back toward the house. Melinda squeaked loudly as he walked away but failed to get his attention. She scurried after him, surprising herself with the agility her little body could manage, calling out to him in her squeaky voice again and again but he took no notice of the little creature scampering behind him. She was desperate to show off her successful transformation so she didn't give up, running more quickly but failing to attract his attention. He was only a yard or so away from the steps that led up to the back door of the house and Melinda wasn't about to give up the chase so in a last-ditch burst of energy she leapt free of the grass, grabbing hold of the back of his thigh and digging her claws in through his jeans.

Her clothes flew into the air as Felix lunged forward, screeching shrilly as he batted at the rodent clinging to the back of his jeans. Melinda leapt free, ran to a safe distance in front of him and then sat up proudly for him to admire her.

Felix's body was completely rigid as he stared at the creature screaming in front of him. A second later he shook his head. "I don't believe it," he groaned. "What are you?" He took a step closer, bent down and stared into the face of his sister that was now planted on the head of the small rat-like creature. He grabbed her by her furless rat-like tail and lifted her black-feather-covered body into the air until her freckled face was even with his. "You are disgusting," he said, looking like he'd just eaten something extremely sour. He dropped her back to the ground and watched as she rolled to a stop.

"You know what Mom and Dad said, no transforming when Professor Mulligan and Professor Stumpworthy are here!" He stormed into the house, leaving Melinda's clothes strewn about and her with an angry pout on her face. She hated the idea of not transforming but more than that she hated the idea of James Mulligan in her house.

Professor Mulligan, or Professor Walrus as Melinda had always called him because of his full puffy jowls and gray droopy mustache (which actually did make him look like a walrus), had never been her favorite. Felix liked him because he was a scientist. Melinda didn't like him because she thought that he was boring. But the biggest problem for Melinda with having him around was Aesop, Melinda's pet rabbit.

Aesop had been a kind of birthday present to Melinda from Professor Mulligan. Kind of, because when he gave her the rabbit he didn't even know it was her birthday. He simply wanted to get rid of the animal and gave it to the most likely home he could think of at the time. It was only a coincidence that it had been her birthday. She always had the feeling he regretted giving up such a remarkable animal because Aesop could change color.

The first time Melinda had witnessed the change she was surprised but not startled. She had learned in school about animals, like rabbits, that change color to match their surroundings. The first time Aesop changed his color from white to brown, which seemed perfectly normal. The next change was a little stranger. Aesop changed from white to purple with eyes the color of deep red rubies. Aesop could change into an orange bunny or a black bunny or an orange and black bunny. Once he had bright pink polka dots and another time he turned a brilliant daffodil yellow. She tried to show her family what he could do but he didn't do anything when anyone else was around; he was always white with crystal pink eyes. At first it was frustrating not being able to share Aesop's talents with anyone, until she realized that Aesop was probably smart not to. "You are a clever bunny," she had said, "because if my father and Felix knew what you could do they'd probably cut you open and see what makes you tick." She laughed when Aesop responded with a violent shiver.

The day arrived of impending doom in Melinda's mind and of salvation in Felix's. James Mulligan and the imposing figure of Horace Stumpworthy would arrive later in the day.

Elaine was in a state of panic. She wasn't ready. The house had been cleaned from top to bottom, the meals were organized and all of Felix's required documents were prepared just in case. Elaine worried instead about her daughter showing up at the table with chicken feet or worse.

Jake thought Elaine's worries were a bit exaggerated. "Let's give her some credit…she has really controlled her thoughts lately. It's been at least three days with no snouts, antlers, tails, or fur."

That morning Felix had taken refuge in his room, away from his family, to await the visitors. He looked forward to having non-Athenite visitors—real people with whom he could relate. There was still a chance he could attend Professor Stumpworthy's Science School in France. He had been more polite to his family than the previous twelve years of his life; they had to let him go.

At the same time Melinda also sought sanctuary in her room. She was still annoyed about not being able to transform and increasingly worried about Aesop. Then panic swelled up like a balloon as she stroked his azure blue fur. "If you've already changed color in front of Professor Walrus then you might again. And if that happens, he'll want you back to study you." She picked him up and held him nose to nose. "Aesop, you must change back to white and stay that way the whole time he's here. Do you understand?" Aesop wiggled his nose but didn't change color.

She put him back down and thought for a good two seconds before deciding what to do. It was obvious that the best way to talk to him was to become a rabbit. She began by concentrating on his long floppy ears, twitchy nose, cottony puff of a tail, short front legs and strong hind legs. She thought about how his fur felt and how his claws pricked her hands when she held him. She visualized his steady breathing, the rapid flutter of his heart and the gentle grinding of his teeth. Then she concentrated on herself covered in sumptuous fur. She saw in her mind her nose change shape, becoming small and triangular; it was twitching constantly and had long whiskers below. Out of the top of her head she could almost visualize long, floppy, furry white ears but her concentration faltered and collapsed completely as she heard her door open. A quick look at her hands showed that she was still human.

Felix walked in rattling something about the guests arriving soon and that she needed to get ready but as she turned to face him he stopped talking and, with his mouth hanging wide open, just stared at her.

"What do you want?" snorted Melinda, very annoyed at his intrusion.

Felix just stood there, his mouth opening and closing but not making a sound.

"Felix, what's going on?"

Felix continued to stare, his thin lips slightly parted and his glasses slipping down his thin nose as usual. "Your face," Felix snapped angrily. "Can't you control yourself for even one minute?"

Melinda reached up and touched her cheek. There was fur! She felt around her face and realized it was covered with the soft fur she had imagined. She felt a cold slippery nose with long prickly whiskers just below. As she moved her hands up to the top of her head she excitedly expected long ears too, but that part of her felt like Melinda the girl not Melinda the rabbit. *It'll take more concentration,* she thought, then closed her eyes to complete the transformation as if Felix wasn't there.

"You're a freak!" yelled Felix. "You're all freaks and I'm not going to be one of you!" He stormed down the stairs, straight out through the front door and right into the open arms of a tall man who, along with Professor James Mulligan, was about to announce their arrival.

CHAPTER FOUR

"Well, if that isn't an enthusiastic greeting," chuckled the tall, distinguished-looking man holding onto Felix's shoulders. "You must be Felix," he said with a smile, then turned to his companion. "James, you told me how keen Mr. Hutton was to attend the program but I didn't expect such a warm welcome."

Untangling himself from the man's grasp, Felix looked up at the tall stranger with awe. Since his companion was the familiar short, dumpy and disheveled Professor James Mulligan, Felix knew that the man he had ploughed into had to be Professor Horace Stumpworthy. It wasn't exactly the calm and intelligent impression he'd wanted to give at their first meeting.

"I'm sorry I wasn't looking where I was going," Felix stuttered, his cheeks burning red.

"You were in quite a hurry," interrupted James Mulligan. "Are we keeping you from something?"

Felix shivered. *Only escaping from this loony bin,* he

thought. "No, I was just going out for some fresh air. Please come in," he said in a very formal voice. "I'll get my parents."

"No need, Felix, I heard the voices from my office," Elaine said, startling Felix as she seemed to appear out of nowhere.

The sound of voices carried upstairs to Melinda's ears. "They're here!" she shrieked as she patted her furry cheeks and threw a blouse that she had left on the floor over her blue rabbit.

At the same time Jake walked by her room and glanced in. "Melinda," he whispered calmly, "get rid of the hair on your face and whatever else you have that doesn't belong to a human."

She stood up and smiled the sweetest smile that her little rabbit lips could muster. "I'm trying," she lied.

"Good girl," he said, ruffling the hair on top of her head. "When you're finished, come downstairs."

She watched as he walked along the hallway and disappeared down the stairs then clicked her door shut and closed her eyes. After about three seconds, her hands sprang to the top of her head where long floppy ears greeted her fingers. The rest of her was still very human, but she didn't mind. "One step at a time," she sighed happily.

"Aesop, look!" she squealed, holding out her ears to their full eight-inch length. She ran over to her bed and pulled the blouse away from Aesop so that he could admire her ears but Aesop wasn't there. She looked under her bed, then searched every corner of her room, but he simply was not there. "Oh my God," she whispered.

She cracked open her door and listened to the voices of her parents and the two professors fade as they moved to the back of the house. With her face still covered in fur, her little nose twitching wildly and her ears hanging at the sides of her head, she carefully slipped out into the hallway, then quickly and quietly crept down the stairs.

Professor Stumpworthy walked around the living room, looking at the statues and paintings of mythological creatures that seemed to be everywhere. Felix cringed as he watched him scrutinize the weird half-animal, half-human objects, wondering what he would think if he found out that those were the Huttons' relatives.

"These are lovely," Stumpworthy smiled, turning to face Felix. "I'm a big fan of mythological art. As a matter of fact I collect similar pieces."

James Mulligan nodded from where he had made himself comfortable in the big blue chair in front of the fireplace. "Indeed, Horace is well known for his collection."

"Mom's somewhat of an expert on mythology," Felix bragged.

Stumpworthy met Felix's eyes, then turned to face Elaine. "I've heard a lot about your work: connecting facts with fiction. I'm pleased to say that I've read some of your books. Wouldn't it be interesting to find out that some of these wonderful creatures," he said, pointing to a picture of a goat-boy playing a flute, "were actually based on something that was once real?"

"Perhaps they were," Elaine smiled, while Felix looked over nervously.

"Perhaps," Stumpworthy smiled, "I have read some old accounts that suggest that they were."

Elaine walked over to the bookcase that the professor was standing in front of and pulled a volume off the shelf. "It sounds like you've read a bit about the Athena Theory," she said, handing the book to him.

"I have indeed. The theory that there may once have been a race of people called Athenites is marvelous. You can imagine that for a mythology fan like me, references to beings that could take the shape of other creatures would hold a certain fascination." He glanced at Felix, who seemed uncomfortable with the topic. "Now that would be something, wouldn't it, Felix, knowing someone that could transform into something else."

Felix shook his head. "A bit farfetched, wouldn't you say," he said in a cracking voice.

"Of course it is," Stumpworthy smiled. "It would be physically impossible but it would be fantastic if it was true."

"If anyone could prove it was true, it would be Elaine," Mulligan chuckled.

Stumpworthy grinned pleasantly. "I'm quite sure of that. I understand that you have quite a following. It won't be long before people will believe whatever you put in front of them is an absolute fact."

Elaine smiled nervously. "That may be true but I can't say that everyone who reads my research is a fan."

Stumpworthy nodded. "Some people don't like their fantasies reduced to reality. Others might enjoy their skeptical view of the world better than knowing the truth. But as a man of science, I happen to find your research refreshing."

Melinda inched her way down the stairs, hoping that the conversation from the others remained at the other end of the passage. With every step she looked around and whispered for Aesop but it wasn't until she reached the bottom step that she saw his white coat. "Aesop, come here," she called quietly. He hopped away, toward the room where everyone had gathered. Forgetting about everything except the fact that Professor Mulligan was in that room, Melinda lunged forward in an attempt to grab him as he deftly leapt forward into the room.

Aesop sat up, lifted his nose and sniffed the air. He looked from Elaine to Jake to Felix calmly. His ears twitched when he looked at Professor Mulligan, then laid back flat as his gaze rested on Horace Stumpworthy. He lowered himself back onto his front paws, never taking his eyes off of the professor. Grinding his teeth while emitting a tiny low growl he crept slowly, stealthily forward, pausing only briefly before launching himself powerfully at Horace Stumpworthy's upper right thigh. The professor shrieked painfully as Aesop anchored himself by biting directly into his groin.

As blood trickled down Stumpworthy's leg, Professor Mulligan gasped, "My word, what is that thing!" while Elaine and Jake stood dumbfounded, watching their daughter's pet rabbit dangle from their guest's trousers. Felix shrieked for Melinda to "COME AND GET YOUR RABID RABBIT" and Melinda rushed into the room, forgetting completely about her appearance.

Elaine and Jake watched in horror as their furry-faced, floppy-eared daughter raced to the professor's side, wrenched her rabbit off his leg, then darted back out of the room.

Felix wanted to run too, as fast as possible away from the insanity that he had just witnessed. He closed his eyes and wished that he could just disappear, or that his family could—either way, made no difference to him. He felt his prospects with Stumpworthy were over as he listened to what sounded like sobs and coughs and gasps for air. Reluctantly he opened his eyes, then sat bolt upright. Tears were streaming down Stumpworthy's face and Mulligan was gasping for breath but it wasn't what Felix had expected. Both men were laughing hysterically.

"That was the funniest thing I have ever seen," said Mulligan between mouthfuls of food at dinner that evening. "Horace, I have never seen you in such a panic…what did you do to that rabbit before you gave him to me?"

Horace Stumpworthy shook his head. "I have absolutely no idea. Maybe it was something I said," he laughed warmly.

Mulligan turned to Melinda and winked. "What do you think, my dear?" Melinda shrugged then looked over at Professor Stumpworthy and shivered. Mulligan continued, "Now that you know that the rabbit originally belonged to Horace before me, I'll bet you could come up with a reason why the little bunny might attack him."

Melinda smiled and shook her head shyly.

Stumpworthy smiled amiably. "There was no real harm done. Animals often react strangely when their environment changes."

Mulligan nodded. "Come to think of it, I've seen other animals behave strangely toward Horace," he said as he looked around the table. "There is a dog in Horace's neighborhood that would love to take a bite out of his backside, hey, Horace?"

"I'm just one of those people that attracts animals, albeit in a less friendly way than I would like," laughed Horace. He smiled at Melinda, sending goose bumps bubbling up her arm. "What I'm more interested in than my animal magnetism is hearing how you made that superb rabbit costume. I have never seen anything so lifelike—it was absolutely brilliant. Are you going to a fancy dress party or is it for a school play?"

A blanket of silence fell around the table until Melinda winked. "Neither," she said with a giggle. "I'm an Athenite."

CHAPTER FIVE

The smile hadn't left Felix's face for a week. Nothing bothered him, not even Melinda's antlers at breakfast the day before. All that mattered for the moment were the clothes he was stuffing into his suitcase and making sure that he was on time to catch his plane at three o'clock that afternoon.

He was going to study in France and he owed his great fortune to Melinda. After her comment about being an Athenite at dinner during the professor's visit, everything fell into place. The professors had both laughed, causing his parents to relax. It had taken him a bit longer to understand what exactly was happening, but before the end of the evening it had begun to sink in. It was so painfully obvious that he refused to admit that he hadn't understood at first what was going on. His mother had always said that humans cannot accept the supernatural, and therefore they ignore those things and those beings that hold such qualities. In essence, Melinda could have galloped through the room on zebra legs and the professors would not have believed their own eyes.

The rest of the visit had been perfectly relaxed, and in the end he was given permission to attend the Horace Stumpworthy School of Science in Paris.

Felix latched his suitcase and pulled it off his bed, placing it next to another bag by the door. He was finally ready. He looked out the window at the brightening sky then glanced at the clock for the first time since waking nearly two hours earlier. It was nearly six o'clock in the morning.

"Be careful," Melinda had whispered when she had hugged him goodbye at the airport. Although that was nearly ten hours ago, Felix couldn't stop thinking about the edge in her voice and the look in her eyes. Neither was very Melinda-like. It was like she was trying to tell him something important. He had tried to brush it aside; what could she have to say that was especially important? Still, as the hours passed he could not shake the uncomfortable feeling that she did have something ominous on her mind, something that he needed to know but there hadn't been time for her to tell him. "Nerves," he said over and over, "just nerves. What could she possibly know?"

Felix felt the nose of the plane dip down as the seatbelt sign illuminated and the flight attendant announced that they would be landing soon. He pushed his glasses back up his thin nose and looked out the window. In the distance the outline of the

Eiffel Tower was barely visible. Melinda's words finally stopped haunting him.

Felix's excitement was replaced with nervous energy as Stumpworthy's imposing mansion came into view. The huge black iron gates closed behind the taxi as it drove up the long stone driveway, pulling to a stop in front of the thirty-two-room, gray stone palace. Whatever tiredness he had felt after the long flight disappeared the instant he stepped out of the car and looked up the twelve marble steps that led to the massive, elaborately carved wooden front doors.

He pushed his glasses back in place and ran his fingers through his thick brown hair, trying to smooth its normal bushiness, then straightened his trousers and shirt as he began the climb toward the entrance. His stomach churned painfully with each step, and for the first time since leaving his bedroom back in Seattle, he wished that his parents were with him.

He was shown into the foyer, where a manservant named Hector asked him to wait while he announced his arrival. The entryway was easily the size of the Huttons' entire living room and was decorated with the same mythological art pieces that his family owned, except that these were at least a hundred times bigger. In the center of the room was a six-foot statue of Bes, the Egyptian god of mothers and children, with a massive lion head topping its squat body. Felix decided it was even uglier than the one they had at home.

At the base of the stairs was a huge statue of a Minotaur. It was taller than Bes by at least a foot and also more imposing. With the eyes in its bull's head staring down angrily and its muscular man's body poised to attack, Felix felt uncomfortable in its presence.

"Ah, Felix," Professor Stumpworthy's voice boomed as he came into view. "I told you I was a collector of mythological art." He shook Felix's hand, then gestured toward the Minotaur. "They were the guards of the king's fortune. I must say that he is doing an excellent job protecting mine," he laughed as he motioned for Felix to accompany him down a long hallway.

The marble floor of the hallway was covered in brightly colored Turkish carpets, and the walls were lined with more sculptures and paintings depicting half-animal, half-human scenes. If Felix had hoped to escape the constant reminders of his ancestry, it wasn't going to happen here.

Off the hallway on either side were magnificent rooms: a media room on one side and a music room on the other, a study on the left and a billiard room on the right. When they were almost to the end the professor stopped and smiled. "This is my library—my pride and joy and where I spend most of my time." In an *after you* gesture, he stood back and watched as Felix walked in.

Felix's glasses slid back to the bridge of his nose as his head jerked up to look at the stained-glass domed ceiling three stories above the circular room. It was the most impressive place that Felix had ever seen. The first floor was comfortably furnished with three large sapphire-blue sofas and a big leather overstuffed chair positioned around a massive inglenook fireplace. On the other side of the room was a small study with a big wooden desk and chair. Luxurious colorful carpets lay across the marble floor, and bookshelves lined the walls between tall curved windows. A circular staircase at the other end of the room led to the upper galleries, where more books and windows lined the walls. Each of the upper floors opened to the center of the room with low, ornately carved banisters serving as walls.

"I can see from your expression that you like my little sanctuary." The professor grinned as he invited Felix to sit down on the closest sofa. "I'm happy to see that, because we've had a bit of a change with the scheduling at the school." Felix looked nervously over as the professor sat on the sofa facing him. "Don't worry," he said, noticing Felix's expression, "it's only temporary, but we have a bit of a problem with the dormitory that you were meant to live in, so you'll be staying here with me for a while. I've also invited James Mulligan to stay with us for a few weeks; he has work to do at the school and it will be nice to have someone you know here while you get settled in. I hope that's all right with you."

Felix was at a loss for words. He glanced at the thousands of books that surrounded them, then smiled. "That would be great," he said as he adjusted his glasses nervously.

CHAPTER SIX

Melinda's eyes sprang open. Her room was dark except for a sliver of moonlight that shone in through the slit in her curtains. She was wide awake and knew that she would have trouble falling back to sleep, but she didn't care. She was happy to have left that dream behind.

It had been three weeks since Felix had left for Paris and exactly three weeks since her dreams had turned into nightmares. She woke up each night worrying about Felix, her night dress saturated in sweat and her muscles trembling. Night after night her eyes would open with the same foreboding feeling, but because the uncomfortable images of her dream faded immediately, she didn't know why.

The smell of formaldehyde was heavy in the classroom as Felix took his seat. Dr. Harmony Melpot stood at the table in the front of the room, waiting patiently for everyone to sit down. She was a tall young woman with an athletic physique and chiseled features that made her look almost statuesque. Her short blonde hair was always perfectly styled and her dark eyes were uncomfortably intense.

"Good morning, everyone," she said curtly. "In a minute I will ask all of you to come up and choose a bullfrog, which you will be dissecting today."

Felix heard a squeamish moan to his left and noticed that Rupert Merewether's normal rosy complexion had turned green, which along with his shockingly scarlet hair made him look rather Christmassy.

"Amphibians are fascinating creatures," Dr. Melpot continued. "Some have actually been found to transform themselves to survive, as in the case of the Spadefoot Toad."

Felix's hand shot up before he realized what he was doing. "Miss, what do they transform into?" he asked eagerly.

Dr. Melpot arched her eyebrows and met Felix's eyes. "They stay as toads, Mr. Hutton," she said firmly, while the rest of the class snickered. "BUT," she continued with emphasis to quiet the others, "as tadpoles they develop into either carnivores or omnivores depending on the available food supply."

After a short lecture the class focused on the dissection of their toad's respiratory system until the bell rang. "Place your toads inside their plastic trays and seal the lid; we'll examine the circulatory system tomorrow," Dr Melpot announced. In a flurry of activity each student shoved their toad's remains inside their containers, gathered their books and papers, and prepared to leave for their next lesson.

"May I have a word, Mr. Hutton?" Dr. Melpot called as Felix was nearing the door. He turned and smiled sheepishly, still a little embarrassed about his question earlier. She motioned for him to come over to her desk. "I have heard a lot about you from Professors Mulligan and Stumpworthy. I trust that you will be happy at the school and I hope you will feel comfortable in coming to me if you have any questions or need anything at all."

Felix smiled uncomfortably. "Thank you, I will," he said without conviction.

"I mean it, Felix," she insisted. "If you have any problems at all, my door is always open." Felix nodded and turned to go. Then she added, "I have read all of your mother's books."

Felix swung back around to face her. "Are you a mythology fan too?"

Harmony smiled for the first time, making her chiseled features appear less harsh. "I suppose you could say that, but I'm really more interested in truth. My uncle was an archeologist and taught me a lot about the history of civilizations along the same line as what your mother does."

"My mother's not an archeologist, she's a writer."

"What my uncle did with a hammer and chisel, your mother does with a pen." She looked at the confusion on Felix's face. "They both focused on uncovering historical truths. Your mother's work has the potential to open people's eyes and minds about unusual real-life facts previously considered only fairytales."

Felix was beginning to feel nervous and wished they could talk about something else. "I'm more interested in science."

"Science plays a role in almost everything we do, including understanding history. Professor Stumpworthy understands that very well," she said with an almost disapproving grin. "In fact he and my uncle studied at university together: my uncle studied archeology and Professor Stumpworthy science. They became friends because of their mutual interest in uncovering secrets from the past. After they finished their schooling they worked on a few archeological projects together, my uncle using the tools of his trade and the professor, the tools of his. Many of their discoveries were published by the professor after my uncle's death." Again Felix thought that he detected a disapproving tone. "The professor was with him when he died. My uncle's name was Joe Whiltshire." She paused as if expecting Felix to recognize the name. "Ah, I can see that you haven't heard about him. I'm not surprised, although they were friends and Professor Stumpworthy made a fortune by—" She broke off and shook her head. "You might ask him about their work together. I'm sure he will have a lot to tell you," she said with a raised eyebrow.

The fire bathed the library in a golden glow as the first rays of moonlight shone in through the tall windows, giving the room a radiant quality. Felix had completed his homework earlier, and having just located the book about spore fungus that his botany teacher had recommended, he flopped on the sofa across from where Professor Mulligan seemed to have melted into the overstuffed chair.

It was very quiet, with the crackling and popping from the fire the only disturbances, along with the occasional wheezes and grunts from the professor. It was as a library should be but Felix was finding it difficult to concentrate. *Maybe it's too quiet,* he thought. Back home he had learned to concentrate with Melinda's incessant chatter never that far away.

Felix looked over at the professor, who was casually flipping through the evening's paper. "Professor," he asked quietly, "did you know Joe Whiltshire?"

James Mulligan peered at Felix over the top of his newspaper. "I didn't know him, but he and Horace were very good friends. What brings his name to mind?"

Felix shrugged. "I was talking to Dr. Melpot about him."

Mulligan collapsed his paper into his lap. "Ah, yes—Harmony. She and her uncle were very close. In fact I don't think she has ever really gotten over his death." He looked thoughtful for a minute. "What exactly had she been telling you?"

"She said that his work was similar to my mom's."

Mulligan seemed to ponder this for a minute, then nodded. "I suppose it was. Whiltshire worked to dispel old myths about history and your mother tries to explore where mythology and reality are actually connected. Yes, I suppose you could say that it's similar work."

Felix leaned his head against the back of the sofa. "She suggested that I talk with Professor Stumpworthy about the work they did together."

Mulligan squinted, then answered tentatively, "I don't know if that's such a good idea. Joe Whiltshire has been dead for more than six years, but I don't think that either Harmony or Horace have ever recovered from the shock. I always feel there's a bit of tension between them."

"She told me that the professor was with him when he died."

Mulligan nodded. "I think that Horace still feels a sense of guilt about the accident, and I'm afraid that Harmony has a lot of resentment toward him."

"I don't understand," Felix said, nervously adjusting his glasses.

"Putting it simply, I think that Harmony may blame Horace for her uncle's death. You see, Joe fell into a very deep crevice while they were working in the mountains in Turkey. The terrain was very rugged, and after a five-day search, the rescue crew gave up, but Horace stayed for another two weeks trying to find him. Unfortunately they never found Joe's body. Horace, poor man, has had to live with that sense of guilt and grief ever since."

Felix's mouth hung open. "But why would Dr. Melpot resent him for that? He did all that he could."

Mulligan nodded. "Of course he did, but Harmony loved her uncle very much. I don't think that she has come to terms with the fact that it was simply a horrible accident. My personal belief is that her thinking is clouded with bitterness because it was her uncle and not Horace who fell that day."

CHAPTER SEVEN

"Melinda, I can't believe you missed break," Millicent Burbank said, shaking Melinda's shoulder.

Melinda rubbed her eyes and stared into Millicent's chocolate-brown face. Her normally large brown eyes looked exceptionally big. "I did?" she yawned, wondering why Millicent looked bewildered; she had only missed one break, it wasn't the end of the world.

"Melinda, I suggest you try to get more sleep at home, and then you won't feel the need to do so at school," said their teacher Mrs. White, her voice quivering slightly. "And Melinda," she continued, "as you know, costumes and face paint are not allowed during class time. I would like you to go down to the girl's washroom, take off that mask and wash the make-up off your face, then return quickly so that we may get on with our work."

Melinda smiled as she looked up at her teacher whose short, almost white curly hair seemed to glow under the fluorescent lighting; her arms were folded across her broad chest and her expression was a mixture of amusement and displeasure. With a sheepish smile Melinda looked around at her classmates, all of whom were staring at her. Giggles and gasps erupted around the room as she turned her head. Melinda touched her fur-covered cheeks, then rubbed her twitching nose. She stood up calmly and walked proudly out of the room.

She trotted down the hallway to the girl's washroom, ran inside and gasped when she saw her reflection. "Not as good as last time," she groaned, "but it's probably just as well that I only look like I'm wearing a rabbit mask." She closed her eyes and quickly returned to her fully human form, sighing happily at her ability to transform so quickly.

She rubbed her freckled cheeks, then tried to comb through her curly reddish-brown hair with her fingers. "I must have fallen asleep at my desk and dreamt about being a rabbit," she giggled. "At least it was better than the dreams I have at night." Her entire body shivered at the memory.

Elaine looked up from her computer for the first time that afternoon as Melinda told her all about her day at school. "You fell asleep in school," she winced.

"Mrs. White thought that I had a mask and make-up on," Melinda stated proudly. "You should have seen me transform back," she giggled, "just like that," and she snapped her fingers.

Elaine shook her head. "That's not the point. You've been lucky so far. Humans have assumed that you have been in costume. But there will come a time…" She hesitated, shivering at the thought. "I hate to think about it."

Melinda cocked her head and frowned. "You said that they'd never believe it if they saw someone transform—they would assume it was some kind of trick."

"I know what I said, but we still have to be careful; there's no telling what kind of panic we could create." Elaine sighed, looked back at her computer screen briefly before she looked up again. "Tell me more about these dreams you've been having. I think we need to figure out a way to stop them. You're not getting enough sleep."

Melinda shook her head. "I never remember anything about them, but I'm usually worried about Felix when I wake up."

Elaine gave her a motherly smile. "That explains it. It's quite normal to have bad dreams about someone you love when you're worried about them. You need to relax. Felix is absolutely fine and having the time of his life."

"I suppose so," Melinda shrugged, rubbing her hand where Elaine noticed she had a sore.

"What happened to your hand?" she asked casually.

Melinda shook her head. "I must have startled Aesop, because he bit me. It doesn't really hurt."

Elaine raised an eyebrow. "Better have your father look at that when he gets home from the hospital. What's gotten into that animal," she sighed. "First Professor Stumpworthy and now you?"

Melinda could feel the heat rise to her cheeks; she didn't want to tell her mother that this wasn't the first time over the last few months that Aesop had bitten her. "He's just going through a phase, I guess."

Elaine smiled when she noticed that Melinda's big blue eyes were now very pink. "I'm afraid he's not the only one. I think we may need to make some changes with your schooling, just until your spontaneous transformations get under control."

Felix discarded his toad's remains into the large plastic bag being passed around the room for that purpose. He gathered his books with blinding speed, then walked briskly toward the door.

"Mr. Hutton, may I have a word?" Dr. Melpot called before he could step through. He closed his eyes and cringed. He had no desire to have another conversation about her uncle's relationship with Professor Stumpworthy.

He turned quickly to face her. "I don't want to be late for my next class."

She smiled and motioned for him to come to her desk as she glanced at the clock. "You have a couple of minutes. I noticed that you hadn't put your name down to attend the lecture on *The Environmental Impact on the Evolution of Species.*" Her steely gaze bored into him, giving him the uncomfortable feeling that she could read his thoughts. "You had seemed quite interested in the Spadefoot Toad." Felix could feel the heat on his cheeks, and droplets of sweat began trickling down the back of his neck as she continued, "I thought that you might be especially interested to learn about how some life-forms metamorphose to survive."

"Not really," Felix lied, glancing at his watch; his next class was due to begin in exactly eight minutes. "I should be going."

The softness in Dr. Melpot's face was replaced by a stony expression. "Very well," she said, looking down at the papers on her desk.

He waited for a few seconds but when she didn't look up or say anything else, he turned to leave.

"Felix," she said softly, "you must be careful."

He froze in place for only about two seconds before turning to face her. When he did, she was gone; she seemed to have simply disappeared.

CHAPTER EIGHT

Felix's knees went weak. Not more than two seconds earlier, Dr. Melpot had been seated at her desk in front of him. He sucked in a lungful of air, exhaling slowly as he looked around the classroom. The room was completely empty; every table was absolutely clean, including Dr. Melpot's desk. Felix began wondering if he had only imagined the scenes of the classroom less than ten minutes ago: students surrounding the lab tables, poking and prodding their toads' entrails. His knees felt weak; he began to feel sick. Then he noticed a faint line of light slicing through the back wall, just behind Dr. Melpot's desk.

He laughed nervously, remembering that all of the science labs had two entrances: one that the students used to enter from the hallway, another at the other end of the room that led to the teacher's office next door. He looked carefully at the line of light at the back wall and realized that it was indeed a door—a door designed to blend in perfectly with the paneling on the back wall, barely noticeable unless you knew where to look. He shook his head, feeling stupid for never having noticed it before.

He turned to leave, and would have done just that if he hadn't heard his name spoken in Dr. Melpot's office. He wondered if he had been meant to join her. A quick glance at his watch told him that he still had five minutes to get to class. He walked closer to the hidden doorway, leaning in toward the opening. Dr. Melpot was talking softly and rapidly and obviously not to him. He turned again to leave, but could not resist the temptation to hear what exactly she was saying.

"Felix Hutton seems very close to the professor," she said, so softly so that Felix couldn't tell if she was talking to someone else or perhaps simply to herself. "I've got to wait until he doesn't suspect anything." Felix's pulse quickened as he waited for another voice to say something, but the next voice was again Dr. Melpot's. "I've got to find a way to gain his trust." She broke off as a knock sounded at her other door. "Please come in," she announced pleasantly.

With only two minutes to get to his next class, Felix darted out of the science lab and jogged down the hallway. His next class was his favorite—Mathematical Functions and Relations—but today algebraic equations were the furthest things from his mind. He raced into his classroom and took his seat, not noticing the tantalizing equation his teacher had written across the board, or that the parabolic structure prominently displayed at the front of the room was the one that he had designed. The only thing on his mind was, what was on Dr. Melpot's?

Professor Stumpworthy didn't look as worried as Felix had expected after hearing about Dr. Melpot. He motioned for Felix to sit down on one of the brown leather chairs that faced his desk. The professor's office was situated at the back of the school, with tall windows looking out across a park-like setting. The room was richly appointed with oriental rugs on the marble floor; exotic tapestries hung on one wall opposite a built-in bookshelf on another, with more of the professor's collection of mythological statues displayed amongst the books.

"You mustn't be too harsh in your judgment of Harmony," he smiled. "The last few years have been very difficult for her. You see, her parents died in an accident a few years before her uncle died, leaving her completely alone in the world."

Stumpworthy leaned back in his chair and sighed. "When Joe Whiltshire died, we both lost someone very important in our lives." He stood up, turned and looked out of the window to collect himself. When he turned back, Felix noticed the pain in his eyes. "I hope that Harmony will learn to accept that although we miss him, her uncle died doing what he loved best. That is more than I can say about so many people who have never found their true purpose on this planet. But it is hard, I know—I've struggled with his loss as a friend, as well as the loss of someone who could have contributed so much to the world."

Felix frowned. "But Professor, she said that she needed to gain my trust. Why me?"

"Only she knows the answer to that," the professor said, shaking his head, "but she obviously thinks highly of you or she wouldn't waste her time. Harmony is a perfectionist and is only interested in things that she considers worthy of her interest. Maybe you should be flattered."

Felix's face began to take on a crimson glow. "But she told me to be careful. Careful of what?"

Stumpworthy shook his head. "Ever since Joe's death, Harmony has been a little bit paranoid about all the dangers we face every day: crossing the street, driving in a car or flying in a plane. I think the fact that her uncle, who had climbed mountains before, had fallen to his death in a climbing accident has pointed out how precarious life can be. I've suggested she get some help to get though this, but she's a stubborn woman." He walked around his desk and rested his hand on Felix's shoulder. "My guess would be that Harmony sees herself in you: she's alone and right now you are too. My bet is that she's feeling a little maternal right now and wants to make sure that you're safe so that you need never feel the terrible loneliness that has been such a big part of her life."

He looked up at the grandfather clock that stood in the corner of the room. "It looks like it's almost time for your next class." The professor cleared his throat and continued. "I almost forgot to tell you, you'll be moving into the dormitory in a couple of days. I must admit that the house will seem a bit empty without you, but you'll probably have a lot more fun with people your own age. And remember, I'm only a phone call away if you need anything." Felix nodded and began walking toward the door. "Oh, Felix," the professor continued in almost an apologetic tone, "the teacher in charge of your wing will be Dr. Melpot. I hope that won't be a problem."

Felix cringed as he left Stumpworthy's office, feeling trapped and alone. He didn't want to spend any more time with Dr. Harmony Melpot than was absolutely necessary, and now he learned that he would be just about living under the same roof with her!

He walked angrily down the hallway, rounded the corner, and then stopped abruptly when he heard the raised voices of Dr. Melpot and Professor Mulligan coming from Dr. Melpot's office. A second later, Professor Mulligan stormed into the hallway, looking unusually agitated. As he waddled past, Felix heard him muttering "Impossible woman" under his breath.

CHAPTER NINE

Melinda's face glistened in the sun; her swollen eyes squinted against the blinding light. Aesop had run out through the back door and into the garden more than six hours ago. He hadn't come when she called. He hadn't responded to the fresh carrots she laid along the perimeter of the garden. He had simply vanished. Melinda couldn't stop crying.

"He obviously wanted his freedom," Elaine said, trying to soothe her. "Just think how you would feel, especially now that you know what it's like to be an animal."

Melinda nodded through huge sobs. "But he was my friend. Why would he run away?"

Jake wrapped his arm around her shoulder and hugged her gently. "He's an animal first, your friend second. He didn't run away, he simply wanted to find a nice lady rabbit and have a family," he said with a sad smile. He was glad that she couldn't read his mind, as he was sure that the poor bunny had become dinner for a local fox or coyote.

Melinda smiled sadly. "He was my *only* friend."

Felix laid the phone back onto Professor Stumpworthy's desk in the library. He was feeling uncharacteristically sorry for Melinda. Most of her troubles were self-inflicted and he usually had no sympathy for her no matter what she had gotten herself into. But losing her only pet was harsh.

Professor Stumpworthy looked concerned. "Felix, is something wrong?"

Felix smiled and shrugged. "Something good is happening and something bad has happened. My mom's publisher thinks that her latest book could become a best seller. She told her that it should knock the historical world on its bum," he said with a chuckle. His smile melted as he continued, "The bad thing is that Melinda's rabbit, Aesop, is gone." Felix looked over at Professor Mulligan, who was snoring in front of the fire. "He'll be happy about my mom's news, but I wonder if he'll be upset about Aesop."

Professor Stumpworthy flashed a strange smile and shook his head. "I shouldn't think so. James has never been much of an animal lover; that's why he gave Melinda the rabbit in the first place."

Felix turned to face Stumpworthy. "Why did you give it to him?"

Stumpworthy looked a little embarrassed. "To be honest, I thought he might use it as a laboratory animal. I don't really know why he didn't, but it worked out all right. Your sister had a nice pet for a while." He stood up and walked over to stand in front of the crackling fire, staring into the flames for a few seconds. "Tell me, Felix, you don't think the little creature will come to any harm, do you? There aren't any predators in Seattle, are there?"

"We live in the country, so there are a lot of coyotes and foxes. Sometimes cougars come down from the mountains."

Felix watched as the professor's shoulders shook slightly, then in a very strange, squeaky voice he said, "I see. Nature can be cruel at times—but then, life is a bit cruel for all of us occasionally."

Aesop crept out from beneath the hedge as the Huttons' car pulled away from the house. He saw clearly that Jake was driving and Elaine and Melinda were passengers. The car disappeared down the lane and that meant the house was empty.

Eagerly, the rabbit sped across the garden toward the house. When he reached the back door he froze his movements, gradually changing from brown to pink. Then his entire body began to contort. His fur seemed to dissolve and his hind legs grew to several times their original length. His long floppy ears receded then flattened against the sides of his head, and his front paws slowly became hands. Within a matter of minutes a tall, muscular man with gray-streaked brown hair appeared.

Aesop examined his hands, looking at them as if for the first time. He looked at his palms, then at his fingers as he clenched his fists. Laughing in delight, he looked at the rest of his body, shivering slightly.

When he was satisfied with his transformation, he began looking around the back porch. There were about a dozen pots of red geraniums lining the steps. His pulse quickened as he lifted each one. Upon hoisting the eighth pot, a wide smile lightened his expression. Quickly he grabbed the gold key that had been hidden underneath, replaced the pot and, with trembling hands, inserted the key into the lock on the door. He turned the handle and dashed inside.

Aesop trotted through the kitchen and down the hallway, up the stairs and directly into Jake and Elaine's bedroom—more precisely, directly to Jake's closet. He rummaged through the hangers, choosing a maroon button-down shirt and a pair of casual beige trousers. Next, he hurried over to Jake's chest of drawers and withdrew underwear and socks. After dressing, he admired himself in the floor-length mirror by the window; the trousers were snug and a couple of inches too short and the shirt pulled at the buttons. He sat down on the bed with a smile.

He seemed excited and exhausted and slightly confused as he sat there for a couple of minutes, then reached over to a bedside table and lifted the phone. Pausing only to take a deep breath, he dialed a number, crossed his fingers and closed his eyes as he listened to the ringing through the receiver. Finally there was an answer and he sighed happily. "Hello," he said, almost startled at the sound of his own voice. "Could I please speak with Dr. Harmony Melpot?"

CHAPTER TEN

The day arrived when Felix was scheduled to move into the dormitory. Dr. Melpot had volunteered to pick him up and help him get settled; she was due to arrive any minute and Felix was dreading the day ahead of him.

He sighed as he looked out the front windows at the bright October morning. Autumn reds and golden yellows were beginning to mix with the green that dominated the formal gardens. He knew he would miss this place. The professor had promised that he would be back for lots of visits, but it wouldn't be the same as living here. He had gotten used to the splendor of the estate, and the prospect of settling into a room that was about the same size as his closet here left him feeling a little depressed.

After glancing at his watch another depressing thought blanketed his mood: Dr. Melpot would be there soon. Felix would miss his nightly chats with

Professors Mulligan and Stumpworthy as much as he would despise constantly having to avoid Dr. Melpot.

He stepped out through the front doors and filled his lungs with the cool autumn air. The gardens reached out as far as his eye could see, with the distant sound of traffic the only reminder that the estate was in the heart of Paris. Just then a gray flash caught his eye at the far end of the garden—a gray streak that darted across an expanse of lawn in the distance, then disappeared behind a large magnolia tree.

Felix adjusted his glasses and watched as what turned out to be a gray shaggy dog darted across the grass again, then disappeared behind another tree. Seconds later, it poked its head out, looked from side to side, then, in an almost crouched run, crossed the lawn to hide behind another tree.

Felix smiled for the first time that morning as he watched the animal's bizarre commando-style maneuvering. He laughed out loud as he imagined the dog rolling onto its stomach before opening fire with its imaginary submachine gun.

"That's Oscar," Professor Mulligan said, startling Felix as he walked up from behind. "I was watching from the window; you seemed to be enjoying yourself out here so I hadn't wanted to interrupt, but Harmony just phoned and said she'd be here in about five minutes."

The smile on Felix's face disintegrated. He nodded his understanding, returning his attention to the dog Mulligan had called Oscar. "I didn't know that Professor Stumpworthy had a dog."

Mulligan laughed heartily. "Oh my, no. Oscar is not Professor Stumpworthy's. In fact, Oscar doesn't seem to be terribly fond of Horace at all. He comes around here all the time—I think the kitchen staff must feed him. But when he catches even a glimpse of Horace he goes wild, bares his teeth and growls. To be honest I think that the beast would simply love to take a big chunk out of Horace's flesh."

"That's weird."

"I suppose it's another example of Horace's animal magnetism. That dog would sooner grab Horace by the throat than look at him. I've never seen a dog behave like that, but then, I had never seen an attack rabbit either."

Felix laughed briefly before feeling a slight pang of sadness at the mention of Melinda's rabbit. "Why doesn't the professor do something about it— couldn't he talk to the owners?"

Mulligan shook his head. "Horace is surprisingly affectionate toward animals—even when their preference is to cause him pain." He patted Felix's shoulder. "Anyway, it's not our problem, and we have our own concerns—work to do, places to go, or whatever that old cliché is. I'll see you at school on Monday." He trundled back into the house, leaving Felix alone on the front steps.

Seconds later the dog darted out again, running from tree to tree until it was close enough for Felix to see it clearly. Without thinking about his movements, Felix walked down the steps and whistled for Oscar to come.

The dog stopped in his tracks, sniffed the air and began taking tentative steps toward Felix, wagging its tail slowly.

Felix could see that the dog's coat was rough and unkempt; he looked malnourished and frightened. "If only my dad was here," Felix whispered as the poor sickly animal came closer. Tentatively, Oscar inched his way toward Felix—then, as if frightened by something unseen, stopped, lowered his head, bared his teeth and growled.

"It's OK, boy," Felix called nervously at the same time that a stinging pain hit the back of his neck. His eyes rolled up and the ground hit his face before he had even realized that he was falling. He heard the dog yelp painfully…he felt the warmth of the sun… he was aware that he was lying face down on the moist grass, but he was completely helpless to do anything about it.

CHAPTER ELEVEN

Harmony Melpot smiled as she replaced a small picture of a man into the top drawer of her desk, looking up as Professor Mulligan marched into her office. "Please, come in," she said tersely.

Professor Mulligan looked more disheveled than usual. "There's no change, I'm afraid," he said, shaking his head. "Horace has talked with the doctors and has secured Felix's release from the hospital."

"If there's no change," Harmony said hotly, "then why is Horace arranging for his release?"

"You didn't let me finish," Mulligan wheezed. "Since Felix is still in a coma, and doesn't appear to be worsening, Horace has arranged to have the boy moved back into his house. That way, when his parents and sister arrive, they'll be together; after all, the boy's father is a doctor."

Harmony seemed to ponder this for a few seconds. "Do the doctors at the hospital have any idea what is wrong with him?" she asked, tapping her fingers on the desk.

Mulligan shrugged his bulky shoulders. "They don't know for sure, but they're guessing that he's had a rather serious reaction to an insect sting."

Harmony raised a single eyebrow and leaned forward over her desk. "That's what I assumed when I found him lying in the grass…there was a tiny red mark on the back of his neck, like a bee sting."

Mulligan nodded. "I actually didn't come in here to discuss his diagnosis. As the teacher in charge of his dorm, I simply wanted you to know about Horace's plans."

Harmony's eyes narrowed. "Of course," she said curtly. "Horace has everything under control."

Felix would have smiled if he could have when his father lifted his eyelids. He had heard his voice, along with his mother's and sister's, when they came into the room. It was wonderful to see their faces, even if only for a second or two. After Jake had finished examining Felix's eyes, he closed the lids again, returning Felix to the blackness that he had become accustomed to over the last few days.

It wasn't an uncomfortable feeling, but it was one that Felix wouldn't have chosen. He was in a state of absolute relaxation. He didn't feel any pain but he did feel. In fact, he felt everything from the touch of a hand to the jab of a needle. He could hear and, if someone would open his eyes for him, he was able to see, too. The truth of the matter was that even though he was totally paralyzed, he was comfortable. In fact, he had never been so comfortable. He couldn't move a muscle, not even to open his eyes, and for some strange reason he didn't mind. It was like he was in a state of suspended animation where he knew that the world was functioning around him but was not terribly interested in taking part.

The last few days had been very strange. It seemed only an instant after he had fallen onto the grass that Dr. Melpot found him. He had thought about standing up but he couldn't. He tried to speak but he couldn't. He had no idea how he had gotten into such a state and he didn't care.

He was glad to be back in Stumpworthy's house, having not enjoyed the stay at the hospital very much. Being examined by all those doctors left him feeling like he was nothing more than a specimen to poke and prod, much like the unfortunate toads from his biology class. He was glad his father had arrived. He felt confident that he wouldn't be subjected to any more of the hospital's dehumanizing examinations— and maybe, he thought, the daily jabs in the back of his neck would stop.

Melinda stayed with Felix when her mother and father left the room with Professor Stumpworthy. She walked over to his bed, lifted his eyelids, and stared into his eyes. "You're OK, aren't you?" she smiled, feeling certain that he was. The way the adults had been talking she thought that she would look into an unseeing gaze, but Felix's eyes were full of life. They didn't move or respond in any way, but Melinda was sure that he could see.

She smiled, reached up and pulled the big hat off her head, revealing long, pink, floppy rabbit ears. "I got rid of the pink eyes and whiskers," she giggled, grabbing hold of her ears and pulling them out to the side, "but I've had these ever since Aesop ran away. Mom makes me wear that hat all the time now."

Felix would have laughed if he could have. Before he came to Paris, the sight of his sister in this state would have unnerved him, but now it didn't matter and actually seemed funny.

Melinda looked around the room, noticing it for the first time. The massive four-poster bed faced tall windows that overlooked the garden. To the left was the door that led out to the hallway; the room was dominated by a beautiful marble fireplace. The wall it faced had a huge dark brown antique armoire in the center with modern paintings on either side; Melinda wondered if one of them was a real Picasso. On one end of that wall was a doorway leading into a walk-through closet, then into a private green marble bathroom. "Wow, Felix, this place is awesome. Your room is bigger than our whole upstairs in Seattle." She turned back to face him, still holding his eyelids open. "I wish you could tell me what happened to you. Then maybe we could figure out how to make you better."

Felix was so relaxed, he wondered if he even cared.

Harmony Melpot waited at Terminal 1 at Charles De Gaulle Airport. She was early, having arrived a full hour before the flight was due to land. Time moved incredibly slowly. She felt that she had been waiting for days. She smiled, thinking that in a way she had been; it had been three days since she'd received the phone call that had changed her life.

CHAPTER TWELVE

Harmony's eyes seemed to smile as she searched the passengers' faces, wondering if he would still look like the image in the faded photograph that she clutched tightly in her hand. Her heart leapt when any tall, dark-haired man walked into the arrivals hall, but he wasn't among them. Fewer passengers were coming into the terminal now; it was down to a trickle of mostly elderly or disabled people. She wondered if she had only imagined the whole thing, if he wasn't coming. She looked down at her feet, blinking wildly as she tried to stop the tears that were beginning to cloud her vision.

"Harmony," a man's voice said flatly. "New haircut?"

Harmony looked up into his handsome face. "New as of five years ago." She threw her arms around his neck and hugged him tightly. "What took you so long?" She pushed away and looked at him eagerly. "You don't look like a rabbit," she smirked.

He smiled happily. "If you want, you can still

call me Aesop—I'm used to it after all these years. Although, I must admit that I prefer Joe."

Harmony drove out of the airport car park, listening to her uncle's explanation of what had happened to him more than six years ago. "I knew it!" Harmony shrieked proudly.

Joe looked at his niece with a raised eyebrow. "You knew about the virus?"

She glanced at him briefly, then returned her attention to the road. "No, of course not, but I was convinced that Horace was behind your death." She paused, then laughed. "I mean disappearance. Mulligan hates me for thinking that way."

Joe shrugged. "I thought Horace and I were good friends—if the circumstance was reversed and it was Mulligan who had disappeared, I wouldn't have blamed Horace either. Of course, James Mulligan is human, so I don't know what effect the virus has on them." He thought about that for a few seconds, then continued, "After Horace injected me with the virus, I began to transform into all sorts of animals until my body settled into the form of a rabbit. Afterward, Horace explained how the virus works. An Athenite has the natural ability to fight the effects by spontaneously transforming into a creature that has immunity. It can be anything, and for some reason, for me, it turned out to be a rabbit. The effects are meant to be permanent but, as you can see, they weren't."

Harmony glanced at him briefly. "What happened to bring you back to being you?"

Joe shrugged. "Science is your field, not mine—maybe you can tell me."

Harmony smiled. "I'll work on it." She thought for a minute, then looked nervously at her uncle. "Do you think that Mulligan is involved?"

Joe shook his head. "No, Horace hates humans as much as he doesn't care for Athenites who might upset his cozy little setup. The man has made his fortune by using his abilities to manipulate people. Mulligan has never represented a threat and has been a useful source of information because of his scientific and business connections.

"I became a threat when I discovered those hieroglyphs in Turkey," Joe explained. "Those writings could not only prove our ancestral existence, but also prove Athenites had once lived openly in human society. Disclosing that to the world would have changed the course of history, taking mythology out of fantasyland."

Harmony looked baffled. "I don't understand why Horace would be so opposed to the idea. What difference would it make to him?"

"Horace has only been interested in two things since leaving university," Joe snarled. "Power and money. Two things that he has attained only because of his Athenite abilities."

"I still don't understand," Harmony said.

Joe leaned his head back against the seat and sighed. "Horace is fortunate to have the same talent that you have in your ability to understand all animal languages. You are not able to transform, but you can still call upon animal strengths, as well as communicate with any species at any time. Horace has that gift of communication too, and he can transform. For more than twenty years he has used

both of those talents to make himself very rich. He
would first transform into something most people
might not notice, like a fly, then he would sneak into
a meeting where important confidential information
was being discussed about what businesses were
up to. He used that information to choose his
investments in the stock market, which made him an
absolute fortune. That type of activity is considered
highly illegal, and if the authorities ever found out
that's how he made his money, not only would his
personal wealth be wiped out but he could go to
prison for a very long time."

Harmony nodded, then shook her head. "Just
because people would know about Athenites would
not necessarily mean that everyone would have to
live openly. After all, we don't even know who is and
who isn't an Athenite."

Joe glanced out of the window at the people on the
sidewalks and wondered how many of them might be
Athenites. "There are some that can tell an Athenite
from a human just by looking into their eyes. In an
open civilization where Athenites were accepted and
recognized as real members of society, it wouldn't take
long to discover who is and who isn't an Athenite. As
far as I know, no one in our family has had that kind
of recognition power, but some, like Horace, do. I feel
quite confident that he knows about the Huttons."

Harmony slammed on the breaks, causing the
car in back of her to swerve and honk loudly. "The
Huttons are Athenites?"

Joe grabbed hold of the dashboard to steady
himself. "That is precisely why he is so interested in
young Felix."

Several more cars angrily tooted their horns
until Harmony accelerated again. "Felix is brilliant

and Horace is always excited about bright kids that can attend the school."

Joe shook his head. "That's only partly true. Horace has always kept an eye out for exceptionally bright science scholars because he doesn't want them to discover that metamorphosis is a very real scientific possibility. If one of them is an Athenite, how long do you think it would take them to discover the scientific explanation for our existence?"

"Felix did seem interested in the Spadefoot Toad." Harmony pulled the car to a stop in front of a tall seventeenth-century white stone building. "I haven't told you about Felix yet."

"I know a lot about Felix already…need I remind you that I lived in the same house with him for a few years?"

Harmony turned off the engine and turned to face her uncle. "He's suffered an accident and is in a coma."

"Accident?" Joe snarled sarcastically. "Never assume where Horace is concerned. You also need to know that Horace's interest isn't only with Felix. Elaine Hutton has uncovered some of the same types of information as those cave writings described. From what I understand, her work is just about to be published—something that Horace won't be terribly happy to see done. But I don't think that eliminating Elaine would solve his problem, because the publisher already has rights to the book. The only way that book will not be published is if Elaine cancels the publication, and that is something that she would never do." He opened the door but paused before stepping out.

Harmony's eyes flashed angrily. "Joe, get back in. Let's get over there right now and make sure that he doesn't do something horrible to them."

Joe shook his head. "Now that Horace has control of Felix and his family is living comfortably under his roof, he controls the cards. If we make a move, and it's the wrong move, then all their lives could be in danger."

CHAPTER THIRTEEN

Felix listened to all the subtle sounds that disturbed the silence as if they were music. He knew from the quiet that the hour was late. In the hospital, someone had usually come in and given him some kind of injection long before now. He was happy that it wouldn't happen tonight.

For the first time in days he began to feel uncomfortable, like he had pins and needles all over his body. *It's like my whole body is waking up,* he thought excitedly. Seconds passed and his discomfort grew. He was sure that he could feel his hand twitch and he could just about wiggle his fingers.

The door squeaked open and Felix waited excitedly. He would show whoever was there that he was getting better. With all his energy he tried to lift his eyelids.

"Ah, Felix, I see the Burungo is wearing off," Professor Stumpworthy said quietly. "It's the most powerful sedative in the world. Funny, other doctors aren't aware of its unique properties." He sighed happily. "At first I had thought of letting my little virus work its magic, but since you haven't begun to mature, I didn't know what would happen to you—it might actually kill you," he chuckled oddly, "and you being in a coma is much more effective."

Felix listened in horror.

"As planned, your illness brought the rest of your family here. Your father, as a man of science, will enjoy participating in some of my little experiments. However, your mother presents a bit of a problem. I can't very well have her disappear; that wouldn't do any good. I do have other tricks up my sleeve. I'll admit that they're experimental, but they could be very effective. Your little sister may prove a useful tool before I try them out on your lovely mother," he hissed. "And you, my dear boy, are serving your purpose quite nicely…for now."

For the first time since his paralysis had begun, Felix panicked when the piercing pain of the needle stung at the back of his neck. The drug took effect immediately and the panic left as Felix was sent even deeper into relaxed oblivion.

"No change?" asked Stumpworthy as he walked into Felix's bedroom the next morning.

Elaine was sitting by Felix's bedside; she could see the concern in Horace's expression. She shook her head sadly. "Jake said he'll go to the hospital to run some tests."

Horace nodded somberly. "Yes, I've arranged everything. He'll have everything he needs, including a bed should he feel the need to rest while he's waiting for the results. It can be such a waste of time traveling back and forth to the hospital."

Elaine nodded. "He's used to that. There have been times when he's been gone for days because of his work at the hospital."

That's what I was counting on, Stumpworthy thought, unable to suppress the smile that curled his lips.

Jake walked down the steps to the lower ground floor of the mansion to meet Professor Stumpworthy; they would travel to the hospital together. The stairs curved slightly, ending at a magnificent circular room. In the center of the room was an elegant blue-tiled swimming pool with a mosaic of a mermaid on the bottom. A mural depicting an Italian country landscape was painted on the wall that curved along the near side of the pool. Huge marble columns supported the ceiling. The room was like a Mediterranean resort, with brightly colored flowers and tropical palms growing in enormous urns all around. It was hard to believe that this paradise existed below ground level.

Jake put his medical case down and glanced at his watch; they had planned to leave at least fifteen minutes earlier. He looked up, clearing his throat to attract attention. Then a door hidden in the mural-painted wall opened.

"Ah, Jake," the professor greeted. "Please come and take a look at my own little laboratory for a moment. I would have set you up to work here, but

I don't have the same diagnostic equipment that the hospital does."

Jake followed Stumpworthy into a good-sized room with some of the most advanced scientific equipment that Jake had ever seen. "Horace, this is fantastic. I would imagine that you have everything that I need."

Horace smiled. "Then you think you'd like to stay?"

Jake nodded, pushing up his sleeves as if he were ready to get right to work. "Yes, I would. This will save a lot of time. If I do run into a problem, we can still contact the hospital."

"As you wish." Stumpworthy bowed his head.

Jake opened his medical bag and began removing blood samples, Petri dishes and the microscope slides he had prepared. Suddenly he rocked forward, grabbing onto a counter to steady himself.

Horace clicked the door shut and smiled. "Are you feeling all right?" he asked with a strange, almost giddy quality to his voice.

Jake shook his head as if to rattle himself back into feeling better. "Just a bit dizzy. I'll be fine in a second."

Stumpworthy nodded. "I'm sure you will."

Jake fell forward again, now so dizzy that he could barely stand. His skin began to bubble and fur instantly covered his hands and face; his breathing came in short, desperate gasps. He held onto the counter tightly until violent convulsions sent him sprawling across the floor. His clothes tore as his body expanded, then fell away from him as he began shrinking into a mass of writhing animal parts. It was like a war of creatures fighting for dominance as hooves and paws, feathers and fins all fought for control. His body continued to writhe, getting smaller and smaller until only one animal was visible.

Professor Stumpworthy laughed, bending down to lift up Jake's prone gray mouse body by the tail. "Tsk tsk! Who would have thought that you, such a well-respected doctor, would become such an insignificant little vermin in order to survive the virus," he laughed. "Actually I had a hunch that you might, since mice have one of the strongest immune systems to fight this particular strain." He waved Jake's stunned body slowly back and forth like a pendulum. "I've also improved the delivery method. It's no longer necessary to inject the virus directly into a person—it can be released into the air. Since I'm immune, it's perfectly safe." He checked Jake's vital signs, then dropped him into a waiting cage. "I promised Elaine that you would have a bed, and here you are—fresh paper shavings. I trust that you will be comfortable. And when you wake up we can do some other experiments that I think you will find very interesting."

CHAPTER FOURTEEN

Melinda sat up in bed, shivering, tears streaming down her face. She hadn't had a nightmare in more than a week and this one caught her a little off guard. Her eyes darted around the unfamiliar room; then she sighed as she remembered where she was. She leaned back against the headboard, staring straight ahead at nothing in particular, recalling every image, every emotion, every feeling from her haunting dream.

Felix's voice echoed in the hallway. She ran to his room, where he lay motionless in his bed. He was screaming, "Help me! Stop him!" but his lips weren't moving and his eyes didn't open. She leaned over him and lifted his eyelids, jumping backward when she saw that his eyes were gone. She began frantically searching for them, thinking that perhaps they had rolled under the bed. She bent down to have a look when a mouse scampered out of the darkness carrying Felix's eyes. As she tried to catch the mouse, Aesop walked into the room; he was the size of a man. He tapped her shoulder and said calmly, "I had to leave, but I'm here to help you now."

She rubbed her eyes and ran her hands through her hair; her rabbit ears had finally gone. The bedside clock read 2:00 a.m. She pulled her covers tightly around her and was just closing her eyes, slinking down to rest her head on the pillow, when she thought that she heard Felix's voice call for help.

Melinda's feet hit the floor before she had even thought about getting out of bed. She sprinted to the door, turned the handle and crept out into the hallway. It took a minute for her eyes to adjust to the blackness as she stumbled down the dark passage, wondering why no one else was awake—hadn't they heard Felix's cry?

She reached his room, clicked on the light and hurried to Felix's side. He looked exactly like he had in her dream, and her hands shook as she reached for his eyes. She took a deep breath and gently lifted his eyelids, sighing upon finding that his eyes were exactly where they were meant to be. "Felix, are you OK?" she whispered, watching for a sign that would suggest that he could hear her. Fear seized her like nothing she had ever felt before as she stared into the eyes of a person who simply was not there.

Melinda lifted her head and rubbed her stiff neck. She was sitting in the chair by Felix's bed; her cheeks wore the imprint of his blanket. The darkness in the room was cut only by a sliver of sunlight coming in through the part in the curtains. The clock read 6:25 a.m.

She lifted Felix's eyelids and smiled, feeling certain that he was able to see her. "What happened to you last night?" she asked, knowing that he would not answer. "It was like you were gone. It really freaked me out. Your eyes looked vacant, like they weren't there at all." She shivered at the memory of her dream and decided not to tell him about it.

The door squeaked open and Professor Stumpworthy ambled in. "Melinda," he said, only a hint of surprise in his voice. "I see that you're an early riser too." He walked over to Felix's bed and put down a glass on the bedside table. "I had expected to find your mother here; I brought her a glass of orange juice. I want to make sure she gets some nourishment during this difficult period." He smiled kindly as he lifted Felix's hand and took his pulse. "I talked with your father this morning. He's still busy in the lab. We may not see him for a while."

Melinda looked into his eyes briefly, then turned her attention to Felix. "I know Felix is OK," she said proudly.

Stumpworthy's head jerked around to face her. "I'm sure he will be."

Melinda shook her head. "I know he can't move or anything, but I know that he can see and hear things."

Stumpworthy smiled kindly. "I hope you are right." He looked over at the glass he had placed on the table. "Do you like orange juice?" Melinda nodded. "Then by all means you must have this; you must be thirsty and a bit hungry if you've been up for a while. I will make sure your mother gets another glass." He handed Melinda the glass and turned to leave. "You must keep your strength up for your brother and your family. Good nutrition is the best way to do that." He winked, then left the room.

Melinda watched after him until the door clicked shut. She lifted Felix's eyelids again and stared deeply into his eyes. "There's something weird about the professor," she said, comfortable in knowing that Felix was in no position to argue with her. "I know you really like him but he gives me the creeps. I can't stand to look into his eyes. They're so dark. I imagine I see different animals in them—sometimes snakes." She lifted the glass of orange juice to her lips, never taking her eyes off of Felix. Without taking a sip of the liquid, she stood up, walked across the room and marched through his closet and into the bathroom. When she reached the basin she looked into the mirror, wincing at the painful-looking pattern the bed linens had left on her face. Then without another thought, she poured the orange juice into the sink.

Elaine reclined in a chaise longue on the terrace that overlooked the back garden. "Melinda," she whispered dreamily, "isn't it a beautiful day?"

Melinda frowned, looking out at the formal garden, then around at the stone terrace furnished with ornate tables and chairs and huge urns abundant with colorful flowers cascading down their sides. She knew that the scene looked like a postcard from some faraway, beyond-belief palace, but the last thing she would have thought her mother would say, when Felix was so ill, was that it was a beautiful day. "I guess so," she said absently.

Elaine opened her eyes and smiled at her daughter. "Everything is going to be fine, you'll see," she said wearily, then closed her eyes and sighed.

Melinda curled her lips unpleasantly, shrugged,

then shuffled across the terrace and down the five stone steps that led to a rich emerald-green lawn. She walked across the grass to a forest of white-flowering shrubs, finding an archway almost hidden in their mass of branches. The archway led to a cobbled path that took her on a meandering trek through an exotic mix of lacey ferns and forest flowers, ending finally at another lawn.

This lush grassy haven was bigger than the other. It was surrounded by purple and pink flowers and it had a stone patio furnished with huge potted plants, with a table and chairs in the center and an amazing swimming pool complete with its own rocky waterfall.

No sooner had she reached the pool than she was startled by a man's voice behind her.

"Professor Stumpworthy had it designed to look like a natural rock pond, like the kind that you might find in the tropics," said a deep, gentle voice.

She spun around to see the man approaching. She assumed by his clothing that he was probably a gardener. Something seemed familiar about the tall, dark-haired man, although she felt certain that she had never seen him before.

The man stopped, bowed his head, then looked intently into her eyes. "Hello, Melinda," he said with a wry smile.

When Melinda met his gaze her entire body tingled, like she had just been zapped with a mild jolt of electricity. She swallowed hard and looked away.

"I have a feeling that you know who I am," he laughed.

Melinda avoided looking directly at him, moving her head from side to side as if to disagree, but she didn't say a word.

"Go ahead…you can say it," he coaxed.

Melinda looked into his eyes and knew that what she saw wasn't a dream or a fantasy. For some inexplicable reason, she knew exactly who he was. It seemed impossible but she knew—deep in her heart, she knew. It was like she could see more than the color of his eyes when she looked into them... she could see who he was, not just what he was. She searched her mind and felt a strange kind of connection with him, as if she could read his mind. Thoughts that didn't seem to belong to her swirled in her head. "I must have known you were coming because you were in my dream last night." She hesitated. "But you were still a rabbit." She threw her arms around his waist and giggled, "Aesop, I missed you so much!"

CHAPTER FIFTEEN

It hadn't taken long for Joe to recount his story. Melinda took it all in, nodding with a resigned acceptance as if she had known everything all along, even the part about Horace Stumpworthy being a possible threat to her family.

"OK then," Joe said, smiling. "Harmony has access to the lab at the hospital. She'll talk to your father and we can figure out how to handle this. We'll meet here tomorrow—same time?" Melinda nodded seriously. "Try to keep tabs on Horace and take care of your mom. There's probably no sense in telling her anything just yet."

Melinda giggled. "Yeah, she would rip out Stumpworthy's throat if she thought there was even a possibility that he had anything to do with Felix's condition."

Joe nodded knowingly. "I'm afraid that she might well do just that, in which case we would never find out if he is responsible—and if so, what he has done." He hesitated for a few seconds, then smiled sadly. "I'm sure everything will be fine."

Melinda frowned, not trusting Joe's words for the first time.

"Jake, you haven't touched your food," Horace said as he bent down to look through the bars of the cage. "There's no sense going on a hunger strike," he laughed. "I can't do anything to reverse the effects of the virus. I'm afraid you'll spend the rest of your days this way."

Horace walked across the laboratory and picked up a vial of clear liquid. "This," he said proudly, holding it so that Jake could see, "is something very special. I'm doing the field tests now to see how effective it is." He smiled at Jake and shook his head. "I'm getting ahead of myself, aren't I? You don't know what I'm talking about. Let's see—where to begin?" he mused while tapping his temple with his index finger. "Since identifying the properties of the same virus that has altered your shape, I found that I could separate some of its components. Basically, I have isolated some of the things that make Athenites change. By doing so, I have found that specific elements affect specific changes." He laughed softly. "We'll have plenty of time to discuss all of the scientific findings another time, but in a nutshell, I can now control some of the changes an Athenite experiences, limiting them to suit my needs. For instance, I can use it to change only the way the brain works—actually changing a person's behavior, making them more pliable. In other words, I can train them to do as I wish, just as you would an animal."

He stood up and began slowly pacing the floor in front of Jake's cage. "Call it a form of brainwashing if you want, but in this case the results will be permanent, just like your transformation is permanent. Initial results are quite exciting." He bent down to look directly into Jake's mouse-sized eyes. "Your beautiful wife and lovely daughter have been assisting me as my little guinea pigs."

Elaine and Melinda sat at Felix's bedside; it was getting late. Professor Mulligan waddled into the room carrying a small tray with two glasses of water. "Still no change and no word from Jake?"

Elaine shook her head. "Jake will phone when he knows something, but I expect he's working round the clock, catching bits of sleep when he can. He's done it before, and now that the situation involves his own son…" Her voice trailed off. Then a strange smile crossed her lips. "Horace is sure we'll know something soon."

Mulligan's flabby cheeks shook as he cleared his throat. "Horace asked me to bring you and Melinda these," he said, handing them both a small tablet and glass of water. "It's only a vitamin—you haven't been taking care of yourselves, and he's concerned about you."

Elaine smiled. "He is so kind," she said before popping the tablet into her mouth.

Melinda frowned as she took the tablet off the tray, looking at it as if she'd never seen a vitamin before. She dropped it onto her tongue and drank most of the water in the glass.

Mulligan looked at his watch and sighed. "I'll be off to bed now…you two should do the same."

Elaine immediately stood up and followed him; Melinda remained at Felix's side. "I'll go in a second. I just want to be with Felix for a while," she called after them. As soon as the door clicked shut, Melinda bent over and looked into Felix's eyes. "I've got so much to tell you," she whispered excitedly. "But I don't want anyone to hear me so I'll come back later, after everyone is asleep." She closed his eyes and kissed his forehead, turned off the light and left the room.

The room was dark when the alarm clock rang out. Melinda reached over and hit the small button that would stop the noise, noticing that the clock read 1:00 a.m. She shook her head and slipped sleepily back under the duvet. Drool had soaked her pillow by the time her eyes sprang open again. Her bedside clock now read 2:10 a.m. She scrambled out of bed and fumbled with her dressing gown, which had been turned inside out, and then hurried out into the hallway.

Her eyes adjusted quickly to the darkness as she tiptoed down the passage and into Felix's room. Once at his beside, she didn't waste any time before launching into her report. Her excitement grew when she noticed that Felix seemed to have more of a sparkle of recognition in his eyes, and she was quite sure that his eyelids twitched as she spoke. She told him about how Aesop was actually Joe Whiltshire, she told him about the virus and how Stumpworthy used it against Athenites, and she had just finished telling him how Joe thought he might use it against the Huttons when the door squeaked open and Horace walked in.

Felix's eyes remained open even after Melinda had released her grip. He watched helplessly as she transformed with dizzying speed, dissolving into a furry mass and then dropping from view in a white flash. He had listened to her story in horror, completely helpless to do more than scream out in his head. He knew everything she said had to be true; he wanted to tell her what was happening to him. But when the door squeaked open and Melinda disappeared in transformation he knew what awaited him.

Melinda panted under the heavy fabric of her nightgown. Her head felt dizzy after the quickest transformation of her life, leaving her feeling the way she might have if she'd plummeted down in an elevator after the cable snapped. Her heart raced as the floor vibrated with every step the professor took closer. An involuntary shiver rippled along the length of her rabbit-shaped body and a single droplet of sweat trickled down her tiny, freckled human face. She knew that if he turned on the lights he would see the pile of clothing and it would take only a second or two to discover her underneath. But the professor didn't flick on the light as he made his way across the room to Felix's bedside.

"Ah, Felix. I see you're developing a slight resistance to the Burungo," he said with bitterness in his voice. "I will need to increase the dosage. Another night or two is probably all I'll need anyway; your mother and sister should be quite pliable by then. You, however, represent a bit of a quandary. Since you're not maturing as an Athenite I don't think the virus in its original form will work as it does on the rest of your family. As I mentioned, it might even kill you. I thought about testing it on James Mulligan, but if he should die then I would lose a valuable source for information. But don't you worry—I have something in mind. You will just need to be patient."

An eternity seemed to pass before Melinda felt the vibrations move away and heard the familiar squeak of the door as it clicked shut. Then as quickly as she had transformed into a rabbit, she morphed back into her human form; her eyes darted around the room, fearing that the professor was lurking in the darkness. When she was satisfied that she and Felix were alone, she looked into his eyes again—but the life that she'd witnessed only minutes before was gone, replaced by the same unseeing, lifeless gaze she had met the night before.

CHAPTER SIXTEEN

Torrential rain prevented Melinda from spending her day out of doors. Time was passing painfully slowly; it was hours before she was scheduled to meet Joe in the garden. She rehearsed all the things that she needed to tell him a dozen or more times, about Felix's changing gaze and Professor Stumpworthy's visit to his bedside in the middle of the night. She didn't want to leave out a single important detail.

She had planned to watch Professor Stumpworthy's movements in the hours before her meeting with Joe, but he had left the house early in the morning and wasn't expected back until evening. Professor Mulligan had also left for work at the science school. That left her with her mother and Felix.

There was no change in Felix's condition, except that the life in his eyes had once again returned. Her mother, however, seemed very different. She spent most of her time sitting next to Felix's bed, not doing much of anything but staring at him or looking out of the window at nothing in particular. Maybe her behavior was to be expected, Melinda thought, with her son so ill.

At long last it was time to meet Joe, and Melinda pulled on her raincoat, stealthily making her way through the house to the conservatory. She trotted through the magnificent glass-walled room, with its display of exotic plants, trickling fountains and colorful furniture.

"Are you going out?" Elaine sang dreamily from behind her. Melinda spun around to see her mother gliding across the tiled floor toward a sitting area that had been arranged to enjoy the plants in the conservatory more than take in the view of the garden outside. "This is a pretty chair," Elaine stated as she reclined comfortably onto the soft purple floral cushions.

"I thought you were with Felix," Melinda said with a tiny tremor in her voice that her mother didn't seem to notice.

Elaine smiled softly. "I was, but before Horace left for the day he insisted that I spend a little time in this room. He said that the room had a calming effect. It is lovely, isn't it?"

Melinda eyed her mother suspiciously. Over the last few days she had never seen her mother so calm. Was it possible to get even more relaxed? Brushing the thought aside, she zipped up her jacket and pulled the hood over her head. "I just want a little fresh air," she said smoothly.

Elaine nodded strangely. "You have your raincoat on," she said in a resigned tone. "Fresh air will do you good. I would join you but Horace said that I should rest here for a while. He insisted that the room has healing powers."

Melinda couldn't believe that her mother was behaving in such an un-Elaine-like fashion. Her mother was not known to take other people's advice on many occasions, and sitting alone in a room with nothing to do but take in the "healing powers" of the place was something that Elaine Hutton would never do. Melinda shrugged her concerns away and reached for the door handle, smiling as she waved goodbye. "I will be careful and I'll stay dry, *I promise*," she drawled, expecting her mother to add some motherly advice.

Instead, Elaine looked confused. "OK," was all that she said, closing her eyes as if she couldn't care less if Melinda was either careful or dry.

Melinda shook her head as she walked out into the torrent of water. "Stress does some pretty weird stuff to adults," she mumbled as she trotted down the steps, shaking the image of her mother out of her mind as she waded across the waterlogged lawn. By the time she reached the pathway that led to the swimming pool, she was again rehearsing everything she needed to tell Joe.

Just beyond the swimming pool, she saw Joe waiting under a large evergreen tree that had been clipped to look like a giant bell. The ground was completely dry under its thick branches. As soon as she was close enough for him to hear her, she told him all she remembered of what Stumpworthy had said to Felix: that there was a virus that might kill him, and that he wouldn't use it on Professor Mulligan because of something that she couldn't remember, and that *Durango*, or something like that, needed more *postage*, and that she and her mother were going to be *playable*, although she explained that she had absolutely no desire to play anything with that man. She paused, took a breath, then shook her head while looking down at her feet. "I couldn't hear very well because he was almost whispering and I was under my clothes but he must know that Felix can hear him."

Joe curled his lips as he tried to understand what was coming out of her mouth. "Slow down, slow down...I'm not sure I understand what exactly Horace was getting at." He paused and stared at her for a few seconds, shaking his head slightly. "Let me understand this. You were *under* your clothes?"

Melinda nodded. "As soon as *he* walked into the room I transformed just like that," she said with a wink.

Joe pinched the bridge of his nose with his index finger and thumb, massaging gently as if that was going to unlock the code to whatever Melinda had just said. "If you transformed, then how did you understand what he was saying? I'm assuming he was human at the time?"

"Yeah," she drawled.

Joe rocked his head back against the tree and sighed. "And you were a...?"

"Rabbit," she chirped.

He shook his head, resting his confused gaze on her. "Usually when an Athenite becomes another species they only communicate in the language of that animal...unless you were infected with the virus." He paused and stared at her. "It's one of the lovely things that happen," he said with a great deal of sarcasm. "You're trapped in the body of an animal but you can understand everything you hear, and yet you're totally helpless to do anything about anything. It's the worst kind of prison imaginable."

Melinda shrugged and Joe decided to drop the subject for the time being. "OK then—however it happened, it happened, and you heard Horace talking to Felix, but I'm not too sure what you heard can help us right now." He stepped over to the edge of the branches and held his hand out to catch some raindrops. His expression became serious. "How's your mom holding up?"

Melinda shook her head. "She's acting totally weird. She doesn't do much these days except sit around; she didn't even care that I was coming out in the rain. AND she believes everything that Stumpworthy says and does everything he tells her to do."

"That doesn't sound like Elaine," Joe mused as he leaned against the tree trunk. "I was going to suggest that I talk with her, but I don't think she's in a condition to take it all in. What I'm about to tell you could upset her," he paused, "and I hadn't wanted to burden you with this, but we need to take some kind of action and I don't seem to have a choice." He took a deep breath and stared into the eyes of his ten-year-old companion. "Harmony went to the hospital, but your father was not there— nor has he been. After which she assumed that we had the wrong hospital so she checked another. In fact, she checked out all the hospitals in Paris," he paused to take a deep breath, "and your father has not been to any of them."

Melinda didn't want to believe him, but for some reason did. "The professor said he was working to find out what's wrong with Felix."

Joe nodded solemnly. "That's definitely what he wants you to believe, but obviously it's not happening. I'm confident that Horace knows where he is, but I seriously doubt if he'll tell us." He looked toward the house in the distance. "Your mother thinks he's working and she doesn't seem concerned that she hasn't talked with him." Melinda shook her head. "This is all very strange. Do you know what Horace has been up to today?"

Melinda shook her head again. "I was going to follow him around but he left this morning. I don't know where he went."

Joe patted Melinda's shoulder. "I suggest that you transform into something that he might not notice to keep an eye on him in the house. I will try to follow him when he leaves the property and Harmony can watch him at the school." He paused, looking wistfully at the ground. "She was so happy when she found out that I was alive, almost giddy when I arrived in Paris. But over the last couple of days she's been a bit distant. I suppose I should expect that; after all, she is used to being by herself. Having her uncle hanging around all the time must cramp her style." He sighed and kicked a pinecone out onto the lawn before continuing. "It just seems strange to me that after she found out that your father hasn't been working at any of the hospitals, she's buried herself in her work at the science school. She hasn't been too eager to do anything more in connection with Horace, always saying that she has too much work to do and can't handle any more distractions." He paused, shifting his weight from foot to foot, then turned to stare blankly out across the garden. "I understand that she has responsibilities, but yesterday when I brought up Horace's name, she looked me in the eye and said that we mustn't be vindictive and should let bygones be bygones." He shook his head, resting his gaze back on Melinda.

Melinda smiled back. "Maybe she doesn't want to think about bad things right now."

Joe nodded. "You're probably right. I am sure that she will do what she can."

Melinda dozed uncomfortably under the curtains in Felix's room. She had no idea what the time was, only that she had been crouched in her position for a very long time. She had taken the shape of a mouse—at least that's what she had intended to transform into, because it was small enough to go unnoticed and quick enough to avoid capture. But when she looked down at her paws she knew she hadn't got it quite right. Her paws were green and webbed, very much like the feet of the turtle named Abigail that she'd had when she was five years old. Her tail, with its huge plume of brown hair, was a bit too squirrel-like to pass for a mouse. But the rest of her seemed perfectly mouse-like; she had no way of knowing that her own freckled face was neatly planted on the front of, in all other respects, a perfect mouse head.

At the same instant that she had decided to improve her transformation she was knocked sideways as vibrations from outside the room turned into tremors when the door screeched open and then, with what sounded to her like a clap of thunder, shut. Shivering uncontrollably, she poked her head out from underneath the curtains, gasping when she saw Professor Stumpworthy, who was the size of a mountain, move smoothly across the floor. His back was to her as he stood over Felix. "There you go," the professor chuckled.

"By the time the Burungo wears off you'll be as trainable as the rest of your family…if you survive the infection." Then he turned and thundered back toward the door.

Melinda waited only a second before scurrying after him, barely making it through the door before it shut.

The professor glided down the hallway at an incredible speed, his long strides becoming increasingly difficult to keep up with, especially on tiny turtle feet. He walked to the end of the hallway, pausing briefly in front of a bookcase; then in one smooth motion he pulled the bookcase open to reveal a dark passageway. Melinda stayed neatly behind him, her tail almost being caught when the professor pulled the hidden doorway shut behind him. Safely out of sight, he clicked on a light and continued walking purposefully down the drab stone passage that eventually led down two flights of stairs.

Melinda was finding it impossible to keep up, and it wasn't long before she lost sight of the professor. By the time she reached the bottom of the stairs she was out of breath and shivering. Stumpworthy was gone.

CHAPTER SEVENTEEN

Without warning the light went out and the passage was plunged into darkness. Melinda's eyes strained to see what was happening around her but it was no use. Surprised at not having the nocturnal vision of a mouse, she froze her movements so that she could hear the shuffling of footsteps or the squeak of a door—anything that might offer a clue as to what was going on around her—but the only sound she could hear was her own breathing.

The impenetrable darkness surrounded her, making her feel disoriented and dizzy.

She had never been in a place so totally black, without light of any kind, where it was difficult to tell which way was up and which way was down. She was afraid to move but afraid to stay in place as a choking sensation of panic rose up from her stomach and into her throat. Then a faint amber glow, up near the top of the last flight of stairs, illuminated the passageway.

She leapt up with incredible speed to the first step, then to the second, third, fourth, and all the way to the top, but by the time her feet landed on the cold stone, the thread of golden light was gone. *I've got to get out of here*, she thought desperately.

She thought fleetingly about transforming but was too frightened to concentrate. She crouched down low and rocked back and forth while she tried to figure out what to do. Suddenly a warm breeze tickled her face. She shivered involuntarily and continued to rock slowly as the warmth of the invisible wind caressed her body. It seemed to be directly in front of her, so she took a tiny step forward and felt the warm air wash all around her. Another step and the warmth rippled down her sides; one more step and it brushed the top of her head. In only a few more slow steps the breeze was gone and Melinda collided with the wall.

"Warm air doesn't come out of walls unless there's an opening," she said to herself, and began searching the wall with her front paws. The cold stone was solid, but remembering the hidden doorway in the hallway upstairs, she didn't give up. The warm current was gone as she made her way along the base of the wall, first one way, then the other. There didn't seem to be any kind of opening, crack, or hole that would let air come through.

"I didn't imagine it," she snapped. "I know I felt warm air!" She retraced her steps, patting the stone wildly and sniffing for any kind of scent other than the musty smell of the passage. Still she found nothing. Shuffling back to the center of the step, she felt the subtle warmth across her back. She looked up into the blackness—but it wasn't coming from above. The breeze was definitely coming from behind her, which meant that it had to be coming through the wall.

She turned slowly back around, taking a single step toward the wall, then stopped, feeling the warmth center on her face. Another step forward and the breeze swept across her eyes. Two more steps and the air ruffled the hair on top of her head. Her lips curled into a smile and she made her way quickly over to the wall, stretching herself up to reach as high as she could, but the current was gone. Backing away a few paces, she took a deep breath and then sprang up as high as she could, reaching out with her tiny green paws in hopes of catching a deviation in the wall and perhaps finding the opening that was letting in warm air. She found it on her first try, as she grasped a stony ledge and felt the warm current blow across her knuckles. Her hind legs scrambled up to join them and she pushed her body forward through an opening.

A strange steely glow greeted her when she emerged out of the hole and into a colorless room illuminated only by a few tiny lights obscured from view high above her head. It was a large room, sparsely furnished with tall cabinets and a few stools, similar to a kitchen, but she knew from the acrid smell that it was not. She had visited her father's workplaces enough to know that she was standing in a laboratory.

Her heart raced when she thought that this might be the laboratory where her father was working. It made sense, she thought, that this lab was right underneath the house. She scouted along the wall in search of a bed where she hoped to find her father asleep, where he might be catching a few minutes of rest before resuming his work to find a cure for Felix. She scurried along the perimeter of the room but didn't find so much as a chair that might provide a comfortable spot to take a little respite from his work.

She sighed, deciding that she had seen enough for the night and would tell Joe all about her findings the next day. She turned to leave, but stopped abruptly when she heard a small, squeaky cry somewhere above her. She was sure that the sound resonated from on top of one of the cabinets, but it was impossible to tell for sure from her vantage point. Again the cry broke the silence, becoming insistent, almost desperate.

Melinda ran over to a nearby stool and leapt up to the first horizontal rung that ran between the legs. Balancing precariously like a circus performer, she leapt up again to the next rung. The next step was more difficult, as she had to leap upward and outward, then grasp hold of the seat of the stool. Next she pulled herself up as if she were simply climbing out of a swimming pool, swung her legs up to catch hold, and was on top of the stool in seconds. An easy leap from there and she was on the counter.

Sparkling glass vials and shiny silver scientific instruments were everywhere. She wandered along the hard, cold counter in awe of the forest of scientific machinery, illuminated by the lights of the gently purring machines. Making her way through a city of test tubes and across a sea of computer printouts, she saw the enormous silver cage in the distance; sparkling red eyes gleamed in her direction.

As she got closer, she smiled at a gray mouse, squeaking desperately inside the cage. It sat up on its haunches and squeaked, then rose up on its hind legs, grabbing onto the bars as it chattered in a tirade of mouse talk.

It was then that Joe's words dawned on her: *"When an Athenite transforms they can only communicate with that species."* It brought an important question to mind: why couldn't she understand that mouse? The mouse continued to squeak desperately and Melinda frowned at her inability to understand a single thing it was trying to tell her. She looked down at her green webbed turtle feet and knew that there was only one explanation. Looking anxiously around at the implements on the counter, she spotted what she needed and trotted over to a tall chrome cabinet, squinting before braving a glimpse at her reflection.

"I look like a gargoyle," she shrieked when she saw her image. "I'm supposed to look like you," she whimpered, looking over at the mouse. "I can't understand anything you're saying," she explained as she pulled her human ears away from her head, "because I still have human ears."

The mouse stopped chattering and slumped into a heap, the reflection of its red eyes still glowing in Melinda's direction. Then it stood up again, leaned against the bars and reached out desperately toward Melinda, opening and closing its paws as if beckoning her to come closer. It looked so pitiful, Melinda walked closer, and when she was only a few inches away from the cage, their eyes met.

"Dad," she gasped with the same surprised conviction that she had experienced when she had looked into Joe's eyes and saw Aesop staring back.

CHAPTER EIGHTEEN

Melinda's body was shaking as she pushed the bookcase back in place, concealing the entrance to the passageway. It was cold and she was back in human form, therefore quite naked, but that wasn't the reason that she was shivering. She had made the difficult decision to leave her father behind. He squeaked pitifully when she explained, "I don't want to risk Stumpworthy finding you gone—not yet anyway. It'll only be for a little while, just until I can sort things out." The only problem was that she didn't know how to do that.

She tiptoed down the hallway as fast as she could, not making a sound as her bare feet padded along the Turkish rug that ran down the middle of the marble floor. She didn't have a lot of time to save her father, discover what was wrong with Felix and find a cure, sort out her mother, and deal with Professor Stumpworthy. The enormity of the tasks made her eyes bulge toadishly.

Melinda sat in a big pink chair facing the window in her room, not having stirred for hours. She didn't notice the brilliance of the sunrise; she didn't hear the early-morning birdsong, the distant sounds of frenzied traffic or the subtle sounds associated with the household awakening.

Her body was stiff as she stretched and stood up, trying to clear the haze that was settling in her mind. She yawned and made her way out into the hallway, feeling groggy but surprisingly rested as she walked down to Felix's room.

He was lying in the same position as he had been for days. "Felix," she whispered, not expecting anything in return.

Felix opened his eyes and smiled. "Hi," he managed in a raspy voice.

Melinda ran to his side, grabbed hold of his hand and smiled. "You're getting better; that stuff is wearing off."

"Burungo," Felix whispered. "It's a sedative."

"I know! The professor wanted to keep you quiet."

Felix interrupted, "I know. Everything is going to be OK now."

Melinda frowned. "OK?" she barked hotly. "How can you say that? Nothing is OK except you, but I'm not even sure about that."

"What are you talking about?"

"The professor used that stuff to keep you here and he's using something to make Mom do what he wants her to do and he turned Joe into a rabbit and," she paused for emphasis, "he has turned Dad into a mouse!"

Felix's face contorted into a just-eaten-a-sour-grape expression. "You are not making any sense."

"I saw Dad in a cage downstairs in the laboratory."

Felix shook his head slowly. "I have been in every room in this house, and can assure you that there isn't a laboratory downstairs." He looked at her as if trying to make sense out of what she was so frustrated about, then smiled knowingly. "You've been dreaming again, haven't you? Because the only thing that has happened around here is that I had a really bad reaction to a bee sting. The professor gave me the Burungo to help me relax so that my body could fight the infection. He saved my life."

Melinda shook her head. "That's not true!" Felix didn't respond, putting Melinda temporarily at a loss for words. Then she remembered her father's eyes staring at her helplessly out of a mouse's head. "What about Dad?" she challenged incredulously.

Felix shook his head, smiling condescendingly. "Dad's fine, he's working."

"That's just it," she said ominously. "Harmony checked it out and he hasn't been working in any of the hospitals in the whole city."

Felix's eyes widened. "You have talked with Dr. Melpot?"

Melinda shook her head. "No, but Joe told me; he's her uncle."

"Joe Whiltshire? He's dead. Dr. Melpot told me herself."

Melinda sighed. "I told you all about that—Joe was turned into a rabbit by Professor Stumpworthy, so everyone only thought that he was dead."

"Mel, that's crazy. People can't force people to become animals."

"But *he* can—he uses some kind of virus. I'll bet it's the same one he used to turn Dad into a mouse."

Felix struggled to prop himself up on his elbows and looked into his sister's eyes. "I've studied viruses, and I can assure you that they cannot turn people into animals. Not even Athenites," he added in a whisper. "It's scientifically impossible." Melinda seemed on the verge of tears. "Melinda," he said softly, "you have had another nightmare, that's all it is. I know how upset you were when Aesop disappeared, so it's not surprising that you brought him back in your dream. I told you all about Dr. Melpot's uncle's death and now your subconscious has put him in one of your dreams and has brought Aesop back to you. As far as you imagining that Dad was a mouse…" He pondered this for a few seconds. "That's probably because you felt helpless when I was so ill and Dad couldn't do anything to make it better. In all your dreams you or someone you know has transformed into something. It shouldn't surprise you that you imagined Dad becoming a helpless creature, making it impossible for him to help me. It all makes perfect sense when you know anything about the subconscious mind," he said proudly, squeezing her hand. "You're awake now and everything is OK. Nothing has happened and there's nothing to worry about."

Melinda knew that she should feel a sense of relief or maybe even happiness, but she didn't. She shuffled down the hallway, passed her room, and without consciously planning to do so, stopped in front of the bookcase. The vivid image of that bookcase swinging open to reveal a darkened passageway seemed so real; she couldn't believe that it was only a dream. She looked both directions down the hallway, and when she was sure that no one was around, she grabbed hold of the right side of the shelves and pulled, but nothing happened. With more force, she tugged again—but it was no use, the shelves didn't budge.

"Hello, Melinda," Professor Stumpworthy called from down the hallway. "Wonderful news, isn't it?"

Melinda jerked around to face him but didn't reply.

"It was a difficult time for everyone, but Felix has made it through. He's not only very clever, but physically strong as well."

Melinda blinked in response.

He smiled as he stood next to her. "Now everything can get back to normal. In fact, I just returned from seeing that your father caught his flight on time—now that Felix is well on the road to recovery, he and your mother decided it best that he return to work. Felix will continue to recuperate here for a few days before getting back to his classes."

Melinda remained silent even when the professor ruffled her hair and said that he would see her later. She watched in utter bewilderment as he disappeared down the hallway, finding it hard to believe that her nightmare was over.

CHAPTER NINETEEN

Melinda was still standing in front of the bookshelves, staring down the hallway in the direction that the professor had disappeared, when her mother's voice startled her from behind.

"Melinda," she said in the kind of strong tone that she had always used before Felix's illness, "I'm happy to see you out and about."

With a frown neatly creasing her brow, Melinda spun around to face her mother. *You're the one who has been sitting around collecting dust,* she thought, but managed only to say "What?" in a small, incredulous voice.

"You have been at Felix's bedside for days. We've all been trying to get you to go outside and at least get some fresh air, but you didn't want to leave—not even for a few minutes," Elaine said with a warm smile.

Melinda opened her mouth to protest, to tell her mother about the times that she had gone outside, but simply whimpered "What?" again.

Elaine shook her head. "You didn't want to

leave his side; you have been a very loyal sister."

"Then it was only a dream," Melinda mumbled, looking down at her feet.

Elaine put her arm around Melinda's shoulder. "Don't tell me you've had another dream. I thought you were past all those nightmares you were having about Felix before we came here. You and your imagination," she laughed warmly. "Tell you what," she added enthusiastically. "Felix is fine now, he just needs a lot of rest, so why don't you and I go out for the afternoon—a little shopping, maybe lunch, and how about some of that fabulous French ice cream?"

Melinda stared at her mother and realized that she was acting normally for the first time in days. In fact, everything was beginning to feel absolutely normal. She shivered at the memory of the extraordinary events that she had been convinced she had experienced—impossible situations that could really only exist in a dream. She smiled wearily. "Can we have chocolate éclairs too?"

At the end of the day, full of ice cream and pastries and dressed in the newest of French jean fashion, Melinda flopped onto the pink chair by the window in her room. The chair was warm, having been bathed in the late afternoon sunshine that beamed in through the tall windows.

Melinda looked out at the quiet garden, letting her gaze drift across the grass to the hedge of white-flowering shrubs at the border. She had a strange sense of a more intimate knowledge about the garden: the sponginess of the lawn, where the roses were planted, and of what lay beyond the hedge.

"I must have dreamt that too," she sighed as she recalled a pathway that led through a fern forest and ended at another lawn, where there was a tropical swimming pool and a bell-shaped tree. "That's where I saw Joe," she said sadly, remembering her excitement at being reunited with Aesop.

It wasn't long before the shadows lengthened and color faded with the arrival of dusk. Melinda stood up, gave the garden one last glance, and then left her room. She walked quickly and quietly through the house, darting into empty rooms whenever she thought someone was coming. No one saw her as she scurried into the conservatory, then out through the glass door that led onto the terrace. No one noticed the small dark figure dashing across the lawn, disappearing through the opening in the hedge.

She stumbled along a dark pathway that took her through a forest of leafy green ferns, plants that looked almost black in the faded light of the early evening. The pathway ended at another lawn; in the distance was a tropical pool and to the left was a bell-shaped tree.

"If I never left Felix's side, then how did I know about this place?" she whispered angrily. "I didn't dream it, I couldn't have," she insisted as she marched over to the tree.

"Good evening," Joe said from behind her. "I thought I'd come back one more time to see if you might be here. What happened to you today?"

Melinda spun around and met his eyes; Aesop was staring back. She didn't waste any time telling him everything, from finding her father as a mouse in a laboratory to Felix insisting that there was no laboratory, to her mother convincing her that she had only been dreaming.

"You are not dreaming," he answered calmly. "Although I know how you feel. I spent the better part of the day thinking that perhaps I was dreaming." Joe told her about his day and how, after she failed to show up for their meeting, he called Harmony, who hung up on him no less than fifteen times threatening to call the police unless he stopped bothering her. "She told me that her uncle was dead and that I must be a pretty sick person to play such a cruel prank on her."

Melinda shook her head. "Why would she do that?"

Joe shook his head with a bewildered expression that distorted his handsome features. "Perhaps for the same reason that your brother and mother are trying to convince you that you have been dreaming—maybe they believe what they're saying. Horace has done something to them, but I don't know what, how, or even why."

"He wants everyone to do what he tells them to do—that's what he was telling Felix. He said that as soon as the Burungo wore off that Felix would be just like me and Mom."

"Burungo! So that's what he was using." Joe nodded angrily. "But that's just a sedative, it doesn't affect the way a person thinks. He's doing something else to influence their behavior; it's like he's brainwashing everyone. But that's impossible—brainwashing takes a long time. It doesn't happen overnight." He looked at the ground, then into Melinda's eyes. "What about you—why aren't you following his orders?"

"I must be immune to his charms," Melinda

snorted, "and I try never to talk to him because he gives me the creeps. Like this morning when he was telling me about how he helped Dad catch a plane." She paused and the color drained from her face. "If I'm not dreaming, then Dad *is* a mouse."

Melinda's bedside clock read 1:58 a.m. She had watched impatiently while the dial flipped, minute by long slow minute. At 1:59 a.m. she kicked off the covers, her feet landed on the floor and she ran over to the window, unlatched the lock and pulled the panes open. By the time the clock read 2:00 a.m. a small spotted owl had swooped silently into the room.

Quickly she pushed the window closed, then grabbed a pair of her father's trousers, a shirt, underwear and socks that had been stacked on the pink chair and threw them to within a few inches of the owl. Then she froze her movements and disappeared into her pajamas.

At the same time, Joe emerged from the form of the owl, dressed quickly, then lifted Melinda's clothing in search of her small body. He smiled when he saw his young friend. Her transformation into a mouse was almost perfect. She was the right size and the right color, even her feet were perfect. Most of her head was mousey too, including her ears and nose—and if it hadn't been for her big blue eyes and plump, freckle-covered cheeks, she could have passed for the real thing.

Without a word, and with Melinda safely stowed

in his shirt pocket, Joe stole into the hallway, hurried past the bookshelves and silently ran down the main staircase that led to the foyer. He walked slowly past the imposing statue of the Minotaur, standing sentry at the base of the stairs, and then paused briefly to look at the hideous expression on Bes in the center of the entrance hall before making his way into the hall that led to the library.

About midway down the passage, he opened a door, quickly stepped through, clicked the door shut behind him, and then ran down a short hallway toward a single flight of stairs. The passage was warm and bright, softly illuminated by tiny recessed lights at the base of the walls. Joe hurried down the stairs that ended in a circular room with a swimming pool shimmering in the center. On the wall closest to him was a beautiful mural depicting an Italian landscape; in the curved wall directly across from it were three doors.

Joe rushed to the first door, pulled it open and stepped into a darkened hallway. He searched the wall for a light switch, clicked it on, then walked cautiously down the length of the passage, pulling open doors that led to changing rooms, a sauna, a steam room and a gymnasium. He hurried back to the pool area and tried the next door. This one opened to a very large games room, filled with such comforts as a pool table and big-screen TV. Back out to the pool, he walked quickly to the third door, took a deep breath, then pulled it open. His heart sank when he looked inside to see that it was only a service closet that housed all the pool maintenance equipment.

By this time Melinda, squirming uncomfortably, struggled out of his pocket and ran up to his shoulder. Joe hadn't noticed at first, but when her tiny sharp teeth sunk into his right earlobe he did. Grabbing her by her tail, he dropped her to the ground, not terribly gently.

Melinda sat up on her haunches and sniffed wildly, then in a flash of gray fur she scurried across the deck, around the pool and began scratching at the base of the mural-painted wall.

Joe followed, watching as Melinda sniffed, squeaked and scratched in desperation. He ran his hand along the painted wall, finding the tiniest of deviations to indicate that there was an opening. Now that he knew it was there, he quickly found the outline of the door, cleverly concealed in the lines of the painting. Without too much trouble, he located a recessed door handle and opened the door.

Melinda darted into the dimly lit laboratory and ran over to a tall cabinet; Joe stayed close behind. He saw the outline of the cage immediately, bent down, grabbed Melinda, and hoisted her up to the top of the counter. At exactly the same moment, they saw that the cage was empty; its door hung open and nothing remained inside the bars. Before either of them had time to react, they heard a tiny click behind them and, almost instantly, all the overhead lights flashed on.

CHAPTER TWENTY

When Melinda's eyes recovered from the blinding brilliance of the lights, her panic reverted to confusion upon seeing the shadowy figure in the doorway. "What are you doing?" she squeaked loudly.

Felix stood motionless, staring not at his sister or at Joe but at the struggling mouse that was dangling by its tail between his left thumb and forefinger. He looked slowly and helplessly at his right hand, where blood was oozing out of his thumb. "I couldn't do it," he moaned. "It bit me and I couldn't kill it." Melinda squeaked wildly, but Felix didn't seem to notice. "The professor told me to get rid of it," he said apologetically, looking up at Joe. "I wanted to do what he asked; I was going to kill it, but I couldn't." He paused as if mustering up the courage to go on.

Joe motioned for Felix to come closer. "Felix, do you remember what Melinda told you about Aesop?"

Felix didn't move. He just looked up and without surprise asked, "Are you Joe?"

Joe nodded. "Yes, and Melinda is here," he stated calmly, pointing to her freckled face. "And that little fellow," he said, pointing to the dangling mouse, "is your father."

Felix looked again at the mouse, then walked slowly over to the counter and placed it next to Melinda. "I know it is...now. I had a weird feeling," he said hollowly. "I didn't know at first, not when I was going to..." He paused, looking uncomfortable, then continued in a controlled voice, "I know it sounds stupid, but after it bit me everything changed about the way I felt and the things I wanted to do. I know I'm not making sense," he said, shaking his head. Felix watched as his sister and father embraced and chattered in the squeaky language of mice. "The professor wanted me to kill my own father," he stated in a flat tone; his confession made him feel panicky. "Of course, I didn't know it was Dad, but to be honest, I don't think it would have mattered. I would have done anything he told me to do because whatever he said always made perfect sense...at the time."

As soon as the words exited his mouth his pale complexion faded to an alabaster-white, he slumped forward and collapsed onto the floor.

Felix opened his eyes to see Melinda's face not more than six inches above his. She wasn't a mouse; she was human and wearing a white lab coat. Her mouth was twisted into a kind of bemused smirk. He thought for a second that he was lying on his bed upstairs, perhaps still paralyzed from the Burungo. But he could feel a hard surface under his back, not a soft mattress; he could move his head and wiggle his fingers, and when he looked away from Melinda he saw his father, who was also wearing a lab coat, and next to him was Joe. For a fleeting instant he thought that perhaps he was dreaming.

"Felix, wait till you see yourself," Melinda giggled.

"Never mind about that now," Jake said. "First we have to get out of here."

Felix struggled to sit up, pushing Melinda out of the way as he did. He remembered everything, except how he ended up lying on the floor and why his father was human. "Aren't you supposed to be a mouse?"

Jake looked over to Joe then back to Felix. "I think I'm meant to be, but things have changed," he said with the same smirk that Felix had noticed in Melinda's expression. "Maybe you had better take a look at yourself before we go."

He and Melinda helped Felix to his feet, and Melinda led him across the room to the same stainless-steel machine where she had seen her own reflection the night before. Felix looked cautiously at his reflection, gasping and lunging backward when he saw his face. For the most part he was human, but his nose and mouth had the characteristics of a giant mouse.

"I have the virus!" He swung around and looked desperately at his father. "How do I change back? I don't want to spend the rest of my life like this!"

Jake put his hand gently on Felix's shoulder. "You did have a mutated form of the virus that was allowing Stumpworthy to control you, but I don't think that you have the other form. I just think that you're maturing."

Joe nodded. "While you were unconscious we compared notes. You had been bitten by your father while trying to carry out Stumpworthy's instructions. Remember that at that time, he was infected with the virus, while you were still years away from maturing as an Athenite. After you passed out, you began to change into the animal form that was on your mind at the time: a mouse. Simply put, you had begun to move into maturity. At that same time, your father recovered his ability to change back to human form; in essence, he recovered from the virus. When I was Aesop, I noticed sensations returning, the same type of sensation I felt when I transformed…which coincided with the first time that I bit Melinda."

"It wasn't his fault," Melinda defended. "I stepped on his paw…by accident."

Joe nodded. "I felt strange immediately, as if I could transform. But I didn't think that I could, so I didn't try; I didn't want to suffer the same frustrations that I had years earlier. Still, the sensations continued. I didn't know what was happening, but then Melinda said that I had turned pink."

"You started turning all sorts of colours." She looked from Felix to her father and back again. "I told you he did but you didn't believe me."

Joe looked at Melinda and smiled. "As it turned out, I was regaining my abilities. It must have taken longer for me to completely recover from the virus than your dad since I'd had it for so long."

Melinda nodded excitedly. "And after you bit me, I started having all those dreams about transforming."

"You may have even transformed before the horse incident—in your sleep when your imagination could run wild. Maybe not completely, but little things like feathers, antlers or hooves," added her father.

"Because Dad bit you," Melinda joined in excitedly, "you're just like me!"

Felix met her eyes and groaned.

Jake patted his son's shoulder. "Melinda's right. We think it might have to do with the mixing of antibodies between an infected Athenite and an immature Athenite. My saliva and your blood mixed together, which is the same thing that happened to Aesop...I mean Joe, and Melinda. It's the only explanation that I can offer for the time being; you and I can study it later, but right now let's get out of here."

Felix looked at his reflection again. "I'm not going anywhere looking like this."

Melinda shook her head. "You can change back; just think about yourself. That shouldn't be too hard," she added under her breath.

Felix closed his eyes and did just that. Within a few minutes he'd changed back into his human appearance. "I must be cured from the virus now too." He looked up excitedly. "I won't be doing the professor's bidding anymore."

"None of us will," Joe said confidently.

Melinda folded her arms and frowned. "What about Mom and Harmony? They're both acting the same way that Felix was when they had that virus. Who's going to bite them?"

Jake, Felix, and Joe stopped in their tracks and spun around as if in choreography. "After we deal with Stumpworthy, we'll handle that," Jake offered weakly. "I'm sure we can figure out another antidote for the virus."

Melinda shook her head and looked directly into her father's eyes. "Until we do, I don't think Mom will let us hurt her new master."

Felix looked helplessly at his sister, then to his father and Joe. "She's right. I wouldn't have either."

CHAPTER TWENTY-ONE

Elaine sat at the desk in the library with her manuscript open in front of her. Horace Stumpworthy and Professor Mulligan stood facing her. "You're absolutely right, Horace," she said, strangely cheerful. "My research is riddled with flaws. I called my publisher to cancel the publication of the book."

Mulligan looked uneasy. "I really don't understand, Elaine. You've never made these kinds of errors. Are you sure that your research is faulty?"

Elaine looked up, first at Horace, then turned to face Mulligan and nodded. "I'm afraid so. After Horace was kind enough to read through the manuscript and found some disturbing errors, I combed back through the work, and he's right. There is absolutely no way that this can be published. I would be discredited." She again turned to Stumpworthy and sighed happily. "I can't thank you enough. Once again you've saved the day, not to mention my reputation."

With a forlorn expression neatly planted on his face, Horace Stumpworthy sighed. "I'm sorry I found anything at all. No one wants to learn that there is real evidence to prove the existence of mythological creatures more than I do."

Mulligan cleared his throat. "Can't you salvage the research—do some editing and still go to print? When I read through your manuscript it seemed that all your research was in order...perhaps it's just little things that can be corrected."

Elaine shook her head. "I'm afraid not. There is so much wrong with the material that I can't be bothered to try it again. My heart is simply not into it anymore." She looked up at Stumpworthy with a hero-worshipping grin.

Mulligan was obviously taken aback. He gave a resigned sigh. "This is indeed a surprise. Your readers will be in for some disappointment, but there you have it—you have to do what makes you happy."

Elaine smiled at him, then jerked around to face the doorway when Melinda and Felix walked into the room. Her blank expression suggested to Felix that she wasn't interested in seeing them. Melinda had the feeling that she might not even recognize them.

Professor Stumpworthy met Felix's eyes and smiled so wide that light glistened off his teeth. "Thank you, Felix, for taking care of that little problem downstairs." Felix clenched his teeth but kept smiling as the professor turned to face Elaine. "I had a bit of a rodent problem in my laboratory, but Felix helped me to eradicate it, isn't that right, Felix?"

Felix felt the rush of blood sting his cheeks but kept smiling and nodding obediently.

With a gleam in his eye, Horace Stumpworthy nodded back. "Good boy. I knew I could count on you."

Felix breathed in deeply. "Melinda said the mouse looked like our father," he said. He'd hoped to startle his mother, but her expression remained blank and she didn't say a word.

"What an extraordinary thing to say," Mulligan sputtered.

Horace Stumpworthy's smug expression waned only slightly. "Yes, quite an extraordinary thing to say. I take it that it had not influenced your dealing with the little beast?"

Felix took another deep breath and shook his head. "The mouse is gone."

Stumpworthy nodded, failing to suppress the smile that curled his lips until Jake Hutton walked into the room.

"Yes, Horace, the mouse is gone," Jake said happily, looking at Elaine's blank expression, then at Mulligan, who stuttered, "Jake! When did you get back?"

Jake didn't answer, turning instead to Stumpworthy. "Horace, you don't seem at all surprised to see me. I would have thought that you of all people would be a little startled by my reappearance."

Stumpworthy chuckled softly. "Oh, but I am. You must let me in on your little secret—after all, you know many of mine."

Mulligan patted his brow, which was now damp with perspiration. "You two seem to be talking in code. What are these secrets you're talking about?" Mulligan began mopping his forehead, which was not just wet, but had also become chalky white. He staggered over to his favorite chair by the fireplace and collapsed onto it.

Stumpworthy looked on with a pitying expression. "Poor James," he said, shaking his head, "you don't look at all well. Perhaps you've come down with some kind of virus."

Professor Mulligan didn't seem to hear as his head fell back against the chair. His skin was very sallow, sweat cascaded down his face and his breathing quickened.

Jake hurried to his side, took hold of his wrist to take his pulse, then turned angrily to face Stumpworthy. "What have you done to him?"

At that, Elaine stood up and walked over to Stumpworthy's side. Her eyes flashed angrily at her husband, making her look a bit like a guard dog ready to defend her master.

"It's all right, Elaine, he's not going to do anything," Stumpworthy said calmly. Then he turned to face Jake. "James Mulligan has proven to be a bit of a failure—I had thought that after my success with young Felix and my dear colleague Dr. Melpot that I had eliminated the risk in infecting a human with the virus. I'm afraid my assumption was incorrect. Now it's a matter of wait and see to determine if his constitution is strong enough to fight it or…not."

Felix stepped forward, stopping when he saw the threatening look in his mother's eyes. "You told me that the virus might kill a human!" he yelled. "Why did you give it to him, he wasn't a threat!"

Elaine lunged toward Felix, stopping abruptly when Stumpworthy placed his hand on her shoulder, as if calming a well-trained animal. "What can I say?" Stumpworthy sighed. "As a man of science, I needed to experiment, and had I been successful, the results would have been extraordinary. After all, it worked so well on your lovely mother," he said, patting Elaine again on the shoulder, at which she smiled gratefully, "and I had thought that it had worked on you as a premature Athenite—plus I was very pleased with the results I saw from Dr. Melpot.

It worked beautifully on her, with no ill effects from her human side whatsoever, that I had to take the next step and test it on a regular human. James was the most likely choice. You see, he has been very useful in the past, but I couldn't always count on him, and at times he was a bit slow." He paused briefly, then smiled. "Too bad about him. For you see, if my little experiment had been successful I could have dominated any human I wanted: prime ministers, presidents, royalty—anyone! But never fear…I'll get there in the end."

"I don't think so," barked Jake as he motioned for Felix and Melinda to stand tall alongside him. "I think your days of such experiments are over."

Stumpworthy's head dropped back as a howling laugh exited his throat. He looked at Jake, Felix, and Melinda and shook his head. "Now why would I want to do that? I have no intention of leaving my research, and I'm afraid there is nothing you three can do about it. Elaine is mine and will continue to do whatever I want her to do; that includes defending me against the lot of you."

"I wouldn't be so sure," Joe Whiltshire said as he sauntered into the room.

"JOE WHILTSHIRE!" Horace laughed. "And without your fur coat! This is indeed a surprise. The last time I saw you, you were dangling from my trouser leg. I can't say that I blamed you for your bad behavior, but you did cause a rather nasty bruise on my thigh."

"What a shame," said Joe. "I was aiming a bit higher." Joe walked over and stood next to Jake. "Sorry, Horace, but you are outnumbered, even if you do have Elaine on your side. So I suggest you listen very carefully."

Horace Stumpworthy shook his head pityingly. "I have no desire to listen to any of you. You see, it's not a question of numbers but of cleverness. All of you should know that I never leave things to chance. It is true that your appearance as a human is a surprise. I'm also a bit surprised to see that Melinda and Felix are not affected by the virus. It's all very interesting and something that we really must chat about, but it's hardly a point of concern to my plans." As he was talking he slipped his hand into his shirt pocket, withdrew a tiny syringe, and then, taking hold of Elaine's arm, held the needle against her skin.

Melinda watched as her mother happily let the professor threaten her. "You have already brainwashed her," she shouted. "What else can you do?"

Stumpworthy laughed again. "More than you could ever imagine, my young friend. And although it would sadden me to do it, I am prepared to inject her with wolfbane unless you all do exactly as I wish."

Melinda narrowed her eyes. "What is wolfbane?"

Stumpworthy opened his mouth to explain, but it was her father who answered. "It's one of the few things in the world Athenites fear."

"That is absolutely correct," Stumpworthy laughed. "Please, allow me to explain. Wolfbane is a rare plant found in remote regions of the northern hemisphere. There are a lot of wonderful stories about this beautiful little herb. A long time ago, people, being the superstitious creatures that they are, were frightened of what they thought of as the plant's evil magic. They believed exposure to the plant could turn a person into an animal." He laughed warmly. "Of course, those stories are not true. Wolfbane is completely harmless to humans. In fact, I'm told that it makes a lovely tea. But as with so many old stories about princesses turning into swans and princes becoming frogs, there is some truth to the fable. Wolfbane is only toxic to Athenites. In a way it's similar to my own little virus: exposure to the herb will force a transformation. But unlike my virus, wolfbane forces the person into only one animal form: that of a lemming. And I'm afraid that there is *no* cure to exposure."

No one said a word while the professor gloated with Elaine smiling innocently at his side. Professor Mulligan squinted and listened in stupefaction, but he was unable to do anything about anything. Jake and Joe looked at each other with helpless expressions. Felix just nodded subtly to Melinda, who winked back.

Everything moved at dizzying speed. Professor Stumpworthy's head pivoted around, but by the time he faced Melinda, a massive frog rocketed out of her clothes, landing squarely on his face. The professor fell backward violently as the frog's sticky feet held on tightly. Reeling from the force of the slippery body that had secured itself onto his head, he released his grip on Elaine's arm and dropped the syringe. Elaine looked from the professor to the falling syringe and back again as if she didn't know whether she was meant to retrieve the falling instrument or pry off the huge, slimy green creature that covered the professor's face.

In that split second of confusion, Felix dove across the floor, grabbed the syringe after its first bounce, and rolled to a stop a short distance away. Scrambling to his feet, he tossed the syringe over to where his father and Joe were standing. Then he reached into his jeans pocket and withdrew two more syringes. He lunged toward his mother and thrust the point of a syringe into the center of her right buttock.

Elaine collapsed onto the floor instantly, giving Felix a clear shot at the professor, who was struggling to remove Melinda's frog body from his face. Felix paused, savoring the moment—then he moved with determination, jabbing the needle into the back of the professor's neck.

Feeling the professor go limp, Melinda released her grip and leapt free while Felix leaned closer to the professor's prone body. "There you go, Professor. Burungo—the strongest sedative known to modern science."

But the professor didn't stay quiet for long. His body writhed and shrank; white hairs exploded out of his skin, covering his entire body. Felix pushed backward as the professor melted into a furry mass. Seconds later all that was left of him was a small white animal now occupying the space where he had fallen. It was only then that Felix noticed Joe kneeling alongside.

Joe smiled as he held up a tiny syringe. "So it really does work," he said in amazement. "Let that be a lesson to all of us to stay as far away from wolfbane as we possibly can."

CHAPTER TWENTY-TWO

"That should do it," Jake said as he pulled the syringe out of Elaine's arm. She had been resting comfortably in her bedroom for the last three days. "That was her third dose of the antidote. We should be able to stop the Burungo soon," he laughed, "but let's have some on hand just in case she still feels a bit of loyalty to Stumpworthy." He crossed the room to where Felix, Melinda and Joe were sitting. "Felix, it's lucky that you found the antidote and all the professor's notes about his experiments in that lab. You would have thought after my imprisonment in the horrible place that I might have had an idea where to look, but I didn't."

Felix shrugged. "The man was my hero...I knew everything about him, including how he thought, so I knew where to look. He would never have hidden something so important in a secure spot—that would be too obvious to someone who wanted to get their hands on it. I knew it had to be in a highly unlikely spot—someplace that most people would never look."

"I still can't believe that he stored it in the coffee maker," Joe moaned. "What if someone had used the pot?"

Felix shook his head. "That would have been highly unlikely; no one else even knew about the lab, not even the servants. I didn't know it existed until he told me to kill the mouse." His cheeks tinged red as he looked guiltily over at his father.

"I still don't understand how you discovered that the antidote was in the coffee maker," Joe pressed.

"First, I knew that there had to be an antidote. The professor had said he was immune to the virus, so he would have had to immunize himself. He was too clever to leave anything to chance; relying on some young Athenite rushing to his rescue was not something he would have done. Then it was just a matter of determining where he would have hidden it."

Jake shook his head. "How did you come up with the coffee maker?"

Felix laughed. "That's simple: the professor didn't drink coffee. It's so obvious when you think about it. Remember that no one knew about the lab but him. So you have to wonder why a man who really hates even the smell of coffee would have had a coffee maker."

"That's true," Joe laughed. "I used to drive him mad at university with all the coffee I drank to get through exams. Harmony said that the teachers at the school weren't even allowed coffee in the staff room because the smell bothered him too much."

Felix looked guiltily at Joe. "How is Dr. Melpot? Is she recovering from her exposure to the virus?"

"She's doing very well, thank you," Joe nodded. "At first she said that her head felt like it was going to explode, which made her act a little like a trapped Tasmanian devil. I'm glad that I only had to recover from being a rabbit—the only side effect I had was getting used to a new diet."

"Speaking of diets, Professor Mulligan's diet isn't suffering," Melinda groaned. "I left him downstairs with egg all over his face. How can he eat so much—there must have been at least a dozen fried eggs on his plate."

"I still can't believe he survived, let alone that he recovered quicker than Dr. Melpot and Mom," Felix said.

"He probably only had a single dose, whereas your mother and Harmony had quite a few. My concern over the professor isn't about his health anymore, but about what he remembers hearing and seeing." Jake sighed.

"Everything," the professor's voice rang out as he walked into the room. "I must admit it was all a bit surreal at the time, but the confirmation of Athenite existence is something that I have always believed was possible. That's why I was so interested in Elaine's manuscript. I've had the same theory for years about the reality of beings that could transform to suit their needs in the environment in which they found themselves. People have always been too eager to dismiss the abundant evidence found in every corner of the globe that supports the Athenite reality."

Felix sighed as he looked around at his family and friends with new respect for them and his ancestry. "I guess being an Athenite isn't so weird after all. But I still don't want to learn to change into anything...just yet. I could end up changing into bizarre creatures like my sister. I mean really, Melinda—frogs are small creatures, not giant green monsters!"

Melinda batted her eyes at her brother, then ran out of the room, returning a short time later with a book in her hand. "While you were ill, I spent a lot of time in your room. I didn't have a lot to do so I looked through some of your books. Most of them are really boring—I almost fell asleep just looking at them—but this one…" She paused in her act of flipping through the pages. "…was pretty cool because of all the animal pictures. I read about that toad that you had marked, but I like this one better." She held up the book to show everyone the picture. "This is the Goliath, the biggest frog in the world. Did you know that it can be more than half a yard long when its legs are stretched out?"

Felix wrapped his arm around Melinda's shoulder, flashing a Cheshire Cat smile. "I didn't know that, but I'm glad you did. It's like my old professor taught me: it's not a question of numbers but of cleverness, and you never leave anything to chance."

Acknowledgments

I would like to thank my agent, Fiona Spencer Thomas, for all her support and friendship.

I would also like to thank all the readers who have helped me see the characters come alive through their eyes.

With special gratitude to my mom and dad, Sam, Ian, Barbara, Tess, Emily, Lawrence, John, Kaitie, Jo, Nick, Kevin, Travis, Charlotte, Chris, and Cindi.

Key to Kashdune

By Claudia White

Coming Soon

CHAPTER ONE

The torch beam searched the walls of the dark and humid cavern. Harmony's hand trembled as the light wavered; the batteries were losing power. Just being in a cave was enough to trouble her. Nothing in her ten years as a doctor and a teacher could have prepared her for this. But it wasn't just the darkness and the silence that made her tense; all her survival instincts were screaming at her to flee. She swallowed the feeling and continued exploring the remains of what had been one of the most extraordinary archeological finds of its day. There was little left since Horace Stumpworthy had removed the hieroglyphs. The mere thought of his destruction of priceless history made her blood boil.

She and her uncle, Joe Whiltshire, had arrived in Turkey less than a month before and were now completing their mission. They had taken most of the month to organize and survey the area where the cave was supposed to be, and when they located it they worked day and night for six days, desperately hoping to find a trace of Joe's earlier discovery. More than ten years before, Joe, who had been working in the area as an archeologist, had discovered the cave after the force from an earthquake cleared the way to the entrance. Inside, the walls had been covered in rich, informative drawings that detailed the existence of Athenites, a race of people that could take the shape of other animals—Harmony and Joe's ancestors. More importantly, the cave drawings told the story of peaceful coexistence between humans and their unique Athenite cousins. But little remained of the hieroglyphs now that they had been removed and destroyed by Horace Stumpworthy.

Harmony tensed again, her animal senses telling her to move, to get out of the cave as fast as possible. She tried to ignore the impulse, but this time she couldn't quiet her fear. She yelled for Joe to run. Joe stood motionless for an instant, trying to understand what Harmony was shouting about. Then the earth above and below them started to shake.

"Get out of here!" Harmony yelled over her shoulder. Her uncle was already running close behind her.

"That tremor could bring the whole place down!" Joe called as they ran toward the cave entrance.

The earth groaned and growled, then shifted again, bringing down a rain of rocks over their heads. Another tremor unleashed stones the size of watermelons that crashed horrifyingly close, sending Harmony and Joe scrambling for safety. Dust clogged the air, blocking out the light through the narrow opening. The brightness of the entrance vanished and they watched as the opening dissolved before them. Only seconds passed in what seemed like an endless nightmare before they were left in total darkness.

♪ ♪ ♪

Thousands of miles away, in North America, eleven-year-old Melinda Hutton waited for the dust to settle before struggling to her feet. Her body transitioned back to her human size, her beak was replaced with a mouth and curly reddish-brown hair again topped her head, but not all of her body responded so smoothly to the change. Feathers still clung to her cheeks, her arms were still shielded inside wings and, although her feet had grown to their full human size, they were still very claw-like and scaly.

Melinda's first flight had been a success; her first landing, nearly disastrous. She had come in too fast and at too steep an angle. She had pushed with her wings as her father had instructed, but the speed of her descent made the movement difficult. Her wings caught the wind, bringing her body up slightly, but not enough and not in time. It wasn't much of a landing; it was more like she was the ball and the ground the bat as she hit the grass, then ricocheted back into the air. Her next confrontation with the earth sent her into an uncontrollable spin and she somersaulted several yards away. It happened quickly but as Melinda felt each bump, spin, and tumble, she wondered if it would ever end.

Transforming into different animals had become almost second nature for Melinda over the past several months. She'd only learned about her Athenite heritage a year before, but she practiced her skills daily. Athenites could take the form of any animal, eventually learning to use the skills of that animal as if they were born to it. All it took was concentration, much like a human learning to walk, throw a ball, or ride a bike. Melinda had gotten quite good at many of her transformations and would have been able to master them all if she could learn to concentrate on what she was doing. More often than not her mind would wander and she would change into an impossible creature made up of different animal parts, like a rabbit with a rat's tail and goat's hooves or a pony with feathers. This beast would often sport Melinda's freckled face and beaver-like smile.

Today her father, Jake, had decided to teach her how to transform into a bird and fly. At the onset, he seemed the perfect teacher because of his calm manner. Nothing ever seemed to ruffle or rile him. This was probably because, as a doctor of human and animal medicine, he had seen things that would make most people scream, cry, faint, or at least cringe. Not Jake Hutton—he always kept his cool. His dark hair was always neatly combed straight back, his dark-rimmed glasses always rested comfortably at the bridge of his thin nose, and he always held his lean body tall and straight. He never showed any of the classic signs of stress no matter what was happening around him. Until his daughter tried to fly, that is.

"Okay then," he had said, biting his lip in frustration, "let's try it again. Unlike a crawling insect or mammal, a bird must be PRECISE." Jake pushed his glasses back in place with a shaking hand. "You can't have a hawk's beak on a sparrow-sized head, huge goose feet and hummingbird wings on a…a…a…" He paused when he realized that he had no idea what type of bird Melinda had imagined when she styled her body. He shook his head and sighed. "You look ridiculous." He paused again as he smoothed his hair back off his forehead. "You'll never get off the ground that way. Don't just think *bird*...picture the one you want to be."

Melinda eyed her father as she tried in vain to put a pout on her beak. She was quite certain that she looked perfectly bird-like. He was right about one thing, however, and that was that no matter how hard she flapped her tiny wings, she could not lift off the ground. She transformed back to human form to begin the process again.

Luckily a kestrel glided overhead then, directly above them. Melinda was overwhelmed by its beauty and closed her eyes, absorbed in the sensations of transformation. Her skin tingled as feathers sprouted; her arms felt light, almost weightless. Her skin tightened and stretched across a bony framework that was light and strong and her arms disappeared inside wings. When the sensations had passed, she opened her eyes and stared at her father's shoes.

Jake felt incredibly relieved as he looked down at the beautiful kestrel in front of his feet. "You did it, kiddo! You made it! You're perfect!" He then closed his eyes and calmly transformed into a slightly bigger kestrel. He looked nervously at his daughter, wondering how this next phase of her education—which was really the most difficult and dangerous—was going to turn out. "Ready then," he said, trying desperately to put a little enthusiasm in his tone, "let's try out those wings."

Melinda felt awkward as she opened her wings. Each was longer and broader than her entire body. She raised them and lowered them slowly, feeling the pressure as she pushed against the air. It didn't take her long to get the hang of it, and seconds later she was airborne. Her flight lasted only a few seconds before she tipped forward and slammed into the dirt, unfortunately beak first. She tried again. This time she propelled herself a little bit higher for a little bit longer before losing her balance.

"That's it," Jake cringed.

Melinda eyed him in disbelief. "Surely this isn't really it!" she hissed, spitting out the sandy dirt that was caked inside her beak.

"Now this time, hold your head up high, tighten your back muscles…like this…and you'll be flying." Jake swung his wings together with precise momentum and rose into the air.

"I can do this," she whispered. "If I can change into one of these things, I can fly too." Intensifying her concentration and using huge whooshing sweeps of her wings, she began to rise into the air. Higher and higher she propelled herself until the house and trees were in the distance.

"That's the way," Jake called with a nervous quiver in his voice. "Now slow down and keep your wings out…just relax and glide."

Melinda did so. Suddenly she felt a freedom she'd never known. It was as if the air was holding her, both pushing and pulling while its gentle massaging fingers rippled through her feathers.

They'd flown only a short distance when Jake called again, "It's time to go back. I want you to watch my landing carefully. It's not as easy as it looks," he said as he swooped gracefully toward the ground.

Melinda followed, plunging down a little too sharply. It didn't feel like flying anymore as she plummeted toward the ground.

"NOW, MELINDA! NOW! USE YOUR WINGS!" Jake screamed at the sight of his daughter's free fall.

That was the last thing she'd heard as she careened across the lawn. Finally resting on her back, she waited for the shrieks of concern from her father. Instead, she heard wails of laughter from her mega-boff thirteen-year-old brother, Felix, who had just returned from his home away from home: the library.

Jake was instantly at her side, and after a quick examination to make sure that she was still alive, he sighed, "Don't worry, Melinda, you'll get the hang of all this without a problem—well, without more problems." Melinda sulkily rolled onto her front, feathers and dust whirling around her head.

Felix calmly readjusted his thick black glasses that, as usual, had slipped down his pointy nose. He was dressed in his favorite black jeans and black T-shirt picturing a winking Albert Einstein on the front. His choice of clothing did nothing to enhance his tall skinny frame. With his bushy dark brown hair topping his head, he looked a bit like an overused rag-mop. "Awesome landing, Mel," he groaned, more convinced than ever that he would never willingly learn the skills of an Athenite, having never suffered even the slightest fantasy about transforming into anything. "I'll go inside and see if you made the six o'clock news," he teased, before spinning around and disappearing inside the house while Melinda had attempted to transform back to human form.

Jake's shoulders sagged as he witnessed Melinda's failed attempt to totally eradicate her feathers and return to her ten-toed human feet. "Melinda, you seem more distracted than usual today. What's up?"

Melinda looked up, then followed her father's gaze to her huge kestrel feet. "I can't seem to concentrate," she sighed. "Ever since I got up this morning, I haven't been able to get Joe and Harmony out of my mind."

"Why is that?"

Before Melinda could answer, Felix came bounding out of the house. "Dad, I just saw on the news that there's been an earthquake in Turkey—right in the area where Joe and Harmony are working!"

Get ready to follow the adventures of Melinda and Felix in 'Key to Kashdune', coming 2014!